Middle-Aged Crazy:

Short Stories of Midlife and Beyond –
The Complete Collection

by

Lynne M. Spreen

Also by Lynne M. Spreen

The award-winning, midlife coming-of-age novel

Dakota Blues

and the sequel,

Key Largo Blues

Middle-Aged Crazy:

Short Stories of Midlife and Beyond –
The Complete Collection

by

Lynne M. Spreen

Middle-Aged Crazy: Short Stories of Midlife and Beyond – The Complete Collection/Lynne M. Spreen – 2nd ed.

ISBN-13-978-1497365254

http://www.LynneSpreen.com

To my beloved family, ranging in age from my mother, who is ninety-two, to my newest grandbaby, who is only seven days old as I type this.

INTRODUCTION

When I tell people I write midlife coming-of-age stories, I often get a blank stare. They don't know what I mean. What is a midlife COA story?

Remember the last time you saw a romantic comedy? Typically, the characters are young and clueless, and the story is about them evolving into adulthood, arriving at the gateway to a lifetime of love, satisfying careers, and a beautiful home filled with the sounds of happy children. Fade out. Roll credits. That's your typical coming-of-age story.

But then what? After the kids are raised, the nest empties, and the careers wind down, what's next? Or as my newly-retired friend once said, "What are we supposed to do now? Die?"

I have a better idea: how about we start over and build another life, as satisfying and wonderful as the first phase of adulthood, but different. How do we do that?

Heck if I know. All anybody ever talks about is youth.

And that's a problem. Personally, I just turned sixty. If I live as long as my parents, God willing, I've got another thirty years ahead of me. That's as long as it took to live the whole first part of my life. What am I going to do with the rest of it – if anything? How much is too much? What are the rules, or if not rules, where are the role models?

Even if you're a relative whippersnapper of forty-something, you've thought of this. Although at your age, you probably don't have time to think about much beyond work, kids, and spouse, because you're stressed out and sleep deprived. Did you know the least happy years of a person's life are from mid-thirties to age fifty? Too bad you're not older.

But I digress. So anyway, midlife COA: the kids will grow up and move out, and when they do, sooner or later you're going to have climb out of that bubble bath, set aside the pitcher of margaritas, and make a plan. No generation in the history of mankind has had the privilege of living this long. After our procreating years are over, we have, if we're reasonably lucky, another whole adult lifetime to fill.

What happens in what some have begun calling "second adulthood"?

Here's what makes sense to me: older people have been through so much, they want to read about themselves, and see how their peers got through it, still standing. Still laughing, even. Still taking a chance, starting a business, starting a second family, or falling in love.

We're asking big new questions now, those that were unimportant when we were in our thirties. Questions that are informed by a new sense of our mortality. Like these:

- Are you braver now or more frightened?
- How are you different from when you were younger, and is that a good or a bad thing?
- What would you still like to learn?
- What amazing skill or strength have you finally mastered?
- Is there anything you've given up on achieving?
- What made you decide that, and are you okay with it?
- How do you move beyond caring about the way our society views age?

This whole idea of life in the second half fascinates me. Beyond falling in love, having babies, establishing a career and bringing home all that bacon, you end up an older person who may not be able to leap tall buildings anymore – except mentally – but you're amazing, nevertheless. And you have questions. Where are the answers?

What happens now? That's what I write about. These twelve stories all feature people over fifty, in some stage of their lives where they're trying to become confident again, figure out how to live, and what the rules are – if they even care.

If you want to read more about life in the second half, visit my website and blog. Reflective of a lack of constraint, I named it Any Shiny Thing (**http://www.AnyShinyThing.com**). It's a happy place where we discuss issues facing people at midlife and beyond. You might also be inclined to take a quick look at another web location, my author page at Amazon **http://amazon.com/author/lynnespreen** (no capital latters) where you'll find my award-winning midlife novel, *Dakota Blues*, and lots of nice reviews, and some photos and other tidbits.

Finally, I'm collecting titles of good books reflecting the midlife coming of age story, and posting links to them on my Midlife Fiction Facebook Page. That location is **http://www.Facebook.com/LynneSpreenAuthor**. Come on by and check us out, either to leave a comment or suggest a book. All I ask is that the story feature a main character who is at least forty, illuminate the experience of living the second half of life, and that it be a work of fiction, unless it's a memoir that meets the first two points.

Okay, enough said. Enjoy the show.

TABLE OF CONTENTS

~ 1 ~

TRUCKER

In the blue cold of late afternoon, Rita set out a row of traffic cones around the eighteen-wheeler to warn oncoming drivers, but of course there were none. Travelers had been advised not to attempt Donner Summit for at least another day. Record snow blanketed the Sierras from Grass Valley all the way to Reno, and the forecast called for more. Even CalTrans workers had locked up their snowplows and gone home. The next twenty-four hours along I-80 would be a trial for anyone foolish enough to be out here.

Bracing against the wind and sleet, she climbed up on the back of the rumbling semi. The wind shook the rig, and she remembered a recent overturn in which a coworker had died.

She removed the padlock from the twin sets of steel chains, and heaved each set to the blacktop. She wasn't built for this kind of work. Her hands were too small, her body too light, and in her late fifties, she was too old. Still, it was better than going hungry.

Rita climbed down off the rig, slipping on the icy pavement. With the dark of afternoon, any moisture on the road was quickly turning to ice on the steep grade.

In the brief intervals between gusts, the forest echoed with chill quiet. Then the wind would come howling through the pines and up the slope, rocking the Peterbilt and forcing the mercury even lower. Rita picked up one set of chains and draped them over her shoulder, wincing at the twinge in her lower back.

Rounding the front of the tractor, she slowed to absorb the comforting warmth of the big Cat-15 engine. Together they'd racked up a hundred thousand miles crossing the U.S., through rain and snow and along the outer edge of some bad tornadoes. On just this trip, she'd barely escaped a white-out coming over the Continental Divide from Denver. The previous owner swore the rig was a reliable workhorse. Rita shrugged the chains to the ground. She had no choice but to trust it to carry her down the mountain and into Sacramento by tomorrow morning. Otherwise, the load would be late, and Rita's well-meaning but strict supervisor would knock her back to hauling livestock.

Now, in the silence of the High Sierra, she shivered. Earlier in the day, the dispatcher told her the Pass would be open, at least until early afternoon. The forecast called for a second storm, a bad one, but not until later –midnight at the soonest. Rita had to take the run. The payment on the rig was due, and she didn't make any money sitting in the yard. And no matter how unappealing the job, it still beat teaching remedial reading to juvenile delinquents.

She'd spent a career at the court schools, and not much surprised her in the way of bad behavior, but this time, it was different. The attack had finished her. His tattoo – a knife superimposed over a naked, bleeding woman – would forever be burned into her mind. Even now, she saw it when trying to sleep.

"Remember the rule?" she had said to her students, all teenaged boys. "The 'e' at the end changes the vowel sound." She looked up. At the back of the room, this new inmate was smiling at her, his incisors peeking out from under thin lips. The kid was a man; he should have been in an adult facility.

Right after that, she had him moved from her class, and in

the days and weeks that followed, she never went anywhere around the facility alone. One day, everybody was busy, and she had to pee. He followed her, locked the restroom door, and punched her in the mouth. Shoved her into the sink and took her from behind, yanking on her hair so she had to watch in the mirror. She remembered that tattoo on his forearm, the arm that wrapped around her neck and cut off her breathing. When she came to, her cheek was pressed against the filth of the restroom floor, and she was spitting out teeth and leaking his fluids.

That was three years ago. Her attacker was in prison now, locked up tight, for a few years anyway. Rita, slowly recovering, was driving a truck – hers; she had bought it last January – from coast to coast and back again, concerning herself only with the vagaries of weather, other drivers, and the logistics of getting her loads to their destination without mishap.

Now, kneeling on the pavement in the approaching storm, the cold steel chains felt like they were going to burn through her gloves. Rita crouched by the wheel on the passenger side where only a guardrail protected vehicles from a sheer drop of thousands of feet. The road on which she parked the rig angled upward toward the summit, and the incline called for her to chock the wheels, but she was freezing, so she skipped that step, working fast, trying not to remember.

After the attack, she couldn't work. Couldn't be in the same place where it had happened; couldn't be anywhere else either, it seemed. She was afraid all the time, and took to carrying pepper spray and a knife, and a gun in her car. At home, a run-down rental in San Bernardino, she kept the doors locked and the shades drawn, and watched the Nature Channel all day.

She managed to hide until her disability pay ran out and she was forced to find a job. A temp agency sent her out on office work, but Rita couldn't take the constant noise and light. She tried night janitorial and delivering newspapers, but her attendance was spotty and the paychecks miniscule. When she couldn't pay her rent, she moved into her brother's house. At first she tried to earn her keep, doing light housework and putting something into the crockpot in the morning, but most days, she took the anxiety pills the doctor prescribed and slept until nightfall. As the sun was going down, she'd eat toast and drink a glass of water, then watch TV until dawn. That went on for months. Finally, she couldn't stand herself.

One afternoon, she handed Ernesto a beer and flopped on the sofa next to him. "Teach me to drive your truck."

He almost spewed. "What the hell you talking about?"

"How hard can it be?"

"Stick to secretarial, *mija*."

"Fuck you."

"No, listen, I'm serious." Ernesto cocked his head toward the rig, out in their driveway. "You know how long the front of the house is? That's how long the load is. And it's heavy. You could be pulling forty tons, easy. You think you can just whip around in that thing? Telling you, the four-wheelers'll get you killed; they're like bees sometimes, swarming all in front of you and you have to brake fast without jackknifing. Whatchu gonna do if some little asshole cuts in front of you?"

"Whatever it is you do, I would do."

"Then under the hood you have seven hundred horses, with ten forward gears and two reverse. And that's just the rig. That's not the road hazards or the weather. And it's physically hard. There's not that many women doing it. The other drivers are mostly men. You won't have any friends out there. I say, forget it."

Rita grabbed his beer and drained it, but his skepticism was justified. She was probably too old to learn anything this daunting and dangerous. And what about her mentals? Hell, she couldn't handle running an industrial floor buffer, let alone a tractor-trailer rig. She'd probably crash and die in a freeway fireball.

"I need a shower." Ernesto took the empty can and tossed it in recycling.

Rita watched it land. At this point, she was so pathetic, she was trading in aluminum cans. But the money wasn't the only thing. Until the kid at Juvie, she'd been a proud, highly functioning member of society.

So: operating a rig? Driving from point A to B and collecting a paycheck still sounded better than cleaning toilets on the night shift at the Holiday Inn, afraid of every shadow, every approaching voice.

At least with the truck, she could lock the doors. Her mouth went dry and her stomach rolled over in a nauseating flip.

The shower stopped. Ernesto went into his room. Five minutes later, he came out, dressed in Levis and a tee shirt. "Let's go."

"Now?"

"Yes, now. I have to work tomorrow."

She ran into her bedroom, threw on some clothes, found some sunglasses under a pile of crap on the dresser, and dashed outside where he was warming up the tractor. The passenger seat seemed airborne, it was so high off the ground. Ernesto put the truck in reverse, and with a great burst of exhaust, the truck began backing out, its twin smokestacks jerking from side to side as the big duelies rolled over the lip of the driveway and into the street.

Rita craned to look out the back window. With no trailer, at this high perch, she could see a good distance. At least she had that.

Ernesto drove to a deserted road near the old cement plant, talking all the way there about the importance of patience and respecting the rules. He stopped in the middle of the street and they changed places. When Rita slid behind the wheel, her arms shook and she couldn't feel her fingers, but with Ernesto's guidance, she got it in gear and puttered down the road into the sun. When he instructed her to make a U-turn, she felt the roll of nausea again, but completed the turn without mishap. Going the other direction, east now, working up through the gears to forty miles per hour, the sun behind her, she glanced in the mirror and grinned.

"Yeah, look at you," Ernesto said.

After that first experience, she went along on short runs, driving whenever they were away from traffic. Twice, Ernesto allowed her to come along on longer runs, and she even parked the fully-loaded rig a few times. At first she was speechless with fear, but then something else sparked in her, a tiny flame that flickered and grew as she turned the wheel, as she felt the motor obey the commands from her foot on the pedals and her hand on the gearshift.

It wasn't just the power and independence of driving. Rita loved the solitude. After a few more runs with Ernesto, Rita enrolled in trucking school, earned her license, and landed a job with an outfit in Los Angeles.

Once on the road solo, she used her CB and discovered a community of fellow truckers to answer questions and teach her about life on the road. From them, she learned to use her seatbelts at night to secure the doors, that fuel could freeze, and that drivers can be poisoned by carbon monoxide, so she bought a detector for the cab. The other drivers teased her once they found out the greenhorn was in her fifties, but out on the road they waved as they passed. One day at a truck stop, an old guy saw her struggling with her tandems. He came over with a hammer and delivered a well-placed whack to the locking pin, solving the problem and teaching her something about machinery. He never said who he was and took off before she could buy him a cup of coffee.

Aside from days like this, when her hands were numb and her bones ached from the cold, Rita loved long-haul trucking. There was so much beauty out on the road, from rain squalls across the Arizona desert, to sunrise in the Florida Keys. One hot day coming down off the Carrizo Plain in California, she thought she spotted a pair of condors circling overhead. Since it was almost noon, Rita pulled over and shut the rig down. She grabbed her binoculars and watched the birds ride thermals above the Central Valley. When they'd become tiny specks in the distant sky, she opened her doors and let the breezes rustle through the cab while she made a sandwich in the back. Placing a lawn chair in the shade cast by the cargo container, she enjoyed her lunch, the silence broken only by the ticking of the cooling motor and the dried grasses undulating in golden waves.

Now, the cold wind howled through the forest, and Rita braced herself against the blast. A few snowflakes landed, and she wondered if she had waited too long to chain up. Her instructor, a man with bleached hair, tattoos and pieces of metal in his earlobes, liked to say that some things could only be learned through experience, and he hoped she would live long enough to learn them.

Kneeling next to the outside drive wheel, Rita spread the links of chain. Nearby, a paw print in the snow spoke of recent visitors. The print bore no claw marks, and it was too big for a bobcat according to what she remembered from teaching science class.

So then it was probably lion.

Her gloves prevented frostbite in the relentless wind, but the chill penetrated through her heavy parka. Wind swirled wet brown leaves around the heavy tires. Downslope, tall pines bent and moaned in the face of the second front. The diesel rumbled, waiting, its power vibrating through the blacktop.

Finishing with the first set, Rita stood and rubbed her lower back. She longed for a hot shower and warm bed. There was a travel center outside Roseville where she could park for the night, get a shower and do a load of laundry. Then she would lock herself in the sleeper cab, fix dinner in the microwave and open a bottle of Riesling from the fridge. Secure in her little nest, she'd check her email and perhaps watch Dancing with the Stars on satellite TV. Night would be spent in the safety of numbers, trucks lined up shoulder to shoulder in the vast parking lot. Sometimes the lot lizards banged on the door of her cab, hoping to ply their trade within. When they saw the driver was a woman, they'd slink away. If the girl looked pitiful enough, Rita would slip her a few bucks through a barely-cracked window.

The gathering gloom told her it was well past three. She returned to the driver's side and knelt next to the wheels. Between gusts, the forest fell silent. Not even a raven showed up to squawk insults at her from the high branches. All the other creatures were smart enough to be out of the weather.

Rita's fingers stopped and she turned her head, the better to listen. Another truck? No, the sound wasn't coming from the road. It was coming from below, the sound of wind roaring through the pines and up the slope toward her. Before she could react, the massive squall slammed broadside into the eighteen wheeler, rocking the rig and knocking Rita under the trailer. Cursing the storm, she reached for an overhead crossbar with which to pull herself back up. But the crossbar had slipped out of reach.

The rig moved six inches.

And then it moved again.

Rita squirreled out from underneath and scrambled to her feet. Eighty thousand pounds of brand-new medical equipment had begun inching away on the icy highway. One foot, two – the rig was sliding backwards on the slick grade, on its way to the edge of the road and the deep canyon beyond.

With a mighty heave and a shriek worthy of Serena Williams, Rita hurled a set of chains toward the truck. The chains arced through the air and landed in a heap behind the sliding drive wheels. The tractor thundered up onto the links, mashing steel into the blacktop as the giant duelies fought for purchase. With one last, great tremor, the rig shuddered to a stop, idling patiently now as snow began to fall in earnest.

Gaping, incredulous, Rita felt her gorge rise. She bent over and threw up.

Hands shaking, she climbed up into the cab and eased the rig forward and off the chains. Then she set the brake, chocked the tires and knelt back down to finish the work, humbled by the fact that negligence could have cost her the load, and probably her life, too, considering that nobody would have come to rescue her. She finished chaining up, retrieved the chocks, and climbed back in the cab.

Thirty minutes later, she took the eighteen-wheeler over the summit's crest and down toward the city. Sacramento was only a couple hours away. The worst part of the storm was behind her, and the road ahead looked clear.

Rita turned on the CB, found a channel, and listened to the chatter, reassured by the easy banter and non-stop smart-mouthing. If she ever got up the nerve to tell about it, what a story this would make. Wouldn't the other drivers love it? They would laugh and make fun of the old lady schoolteacher who almost lost her load, but then they would offer to buy her a beer because they had their stories, too.

~ 2 ~

THE KIRBY GIRLS

The girl found my son's driveway just as I was stepping outside to take my baby granddaughter for a walk. The *Santa Anas* were coming up already, and the wind blew her shoulder-length hair every which way, hiding her face. She was holding a clipboard and I figured she was one of those Jehovah's Witnesses, here to save my soul, but then I changed my mind when I saw she was wearing real short shorts the color of old mustard, and black tights. I bent down to my granddaughter in the stroller, fastening the straps so she couldn't fall out, and I thought maybe she shouldn't be seeing this girl.

The girl got closer, and her face was round, showing her to be a baby herself. Those stockings, though, they were something. Like pantyhose with a pattern in them, and there was a big snag, almost a hole, on one thigh. She brushed the hair out of her face and smiled a big toothy smile. "Hi, how are you today?"

"I'm fine. How're you," I said, thinking now she's probably selling pest control. Turned out it was Kirby vacuum cleaners, but she didn't have any equipment or even a car as far as I could tell. She must have been the advance gal, going around the neighborhood trying to schedule people to get their carpets cleaned. Most likely they'd be done by a fast-talking salesman who's sitting in his office right now doing jack-shit.

I used to work for Kirby, I told her. I did telephone solicitation. That was my first job, after babysitting, while I was still in high school.

Her face about cracked in half she smiled so big. She said she graduated early and this was her first real job, too. "Do you have any advice for me?"

I did have some advice for her, but since I wasn't her mother I kept my mouth shut. I was guessing she's maybe seventeen and a half at the most, about two years older than when I worked for Kirby. I didn't mention the way me and the other girls got treated like meat by the salesmen. I wanted to say, Yeah, go home and put on some long pants. Don't smile so much.

But instead I told her, you're selling a quality product. Be proud of that. Stand up real straight and show them you are confident.

Thank you, she said, and she nodded her head but she was looking at my grandbaby. She said she used to babysit all her brothers and sisters. It was fun but she needed more money.

I wondered about a kid who'd go door to door selling vacuum cleaners, and what kind of home life would let her outside looking like that. We said our goodbyes and she went her way, and me and my grandbaby went ours, but then a few houses later, I pushed the stroller back across the street to her and said, "I have a question."

"Yes?" She probably hoped I'd had second thoughts about getting my carpet cleaned.

"Do you have any Mace?"

Her smile went away. "No, I was going to get some but it's my first week and I haven't had time to buy any."

So I fished around in the back of the stroller and gave her mine, and again I wanted to tell her to wear long pants next time. But how do you say that without scaring her, but I was right.

Nobody's home in this neighborhood during the day so it's like a ghost town, and if somebody wanted to knock you in the head and steal your purse or your baby in broad daylight, they could. You could yell but who'd hear you except the dogs, but they bark all day long anyway and nobody pays them any attention. Thinking about what could happen to her made me sick, but I'd said enough. After I gave her the can of spray, I realized now I didn't have anything, but I'm sixty and I have an attitude toward people, so I'm going to see trouble coming right away. Plus I have good body language. For the rest of the walk, anybody got near me I stood up real straight and glared at them, like just you try something and you'll be sorry, mister.

Back home that night, I told my husband about the girl and how bad I felt for her, and he laughed at me.

What?

You got taken, he said. They put her out there looking helpless so people will want to buy because they feel sorry for her. Or worse.

I told him that was sick, but he went back to watching football like it was no big deal. He used to work at a used car dealership, so even though he's a good man, you see this side of him every now and then.

I got between him and the TV and said, maybe she was used like bait, but I don't think she personally could've been running that game. At least she didn't seem so to me.

She got your Mace, didn't she?

He had me there, but it wasn't like I couldn't go buy another can. Bottom line, I think I did the right thing. At least I didn't have to worry about seeing that little gal's face in the morning paper.

I sure am glad I'm older now. It's tough being a kid. You never know when you're being played.

~ 3 ~

SECOND CHANCE

Susan parked her Lexus on the dirt under the shade trees. Across the street, the Rottweiler slept on the porch of the bungalow where her grandsons lived. A Harley stood in the driveway. She sat for a moment, staring at the house. If she lived there, she'd freshen up the paint, prune the climbing roses, and throw some water on the dead stuff that some might call a lawn.

But it wasn't her decision how other people chose to live.

The drooping tree branches swayed in the summer breeze, releasing their peppery aroma into the warm air. The dog lifted its head and gave a half-hearted woof, then went back to sleep. Usually he was in the back yard, but if that had been true yesterday, this whole sad episode wouldn't have happened.

And why hadn't Matt reacted? Sometimes she wondered if her son-in-law (should she still call him that?) used his brains for anything other than beer selection.

The screen door swung open, and the Rottweiler sat up and wagged its tail. Eight-year-old Davy, wearing a Dodgers' cap and basketball shorts, stepped out on the porch and waved at her. Then he helped J.J., three, down the stairs. Their knobby legs and oversized sneakers kicked up swirls of dust on the unpaved driveway. At its gate, Davy stretched the bungee cord to let his little brother squeeze through. "Hi, Grandma," he said.

Susan hugged them both while glancing at the porch, but neither Matt nor his girlfriend appeared. "Are they home?"

"Dad's out back. He said it was okay if you took us."

"Big of him."

"What, Grandma?"

"Nothing." She scooped up J.J. and nuzzled his blood-scabbed cheek. "How're you feeling, sweetie?"

"Good." The little guy always said that.

"Why don't we start looking on this street?" she said.

Davy set off. "Then if we don't find it, we can cut over to Forty-fifth."

As they began to walk the neighborhood, Susan shifted J.J. to her other hip, an excuse to examine the slash marks on his face and the bite on his hand. Yesterday, he had tried to pet a feral tomcat sleeping in the backyard. The cat, startled awake, reacted in fear, its claws barely missing J.J.'s right eye.

"Did the cat look healthy?" she had asked Davy last night when he called.

"It was real dirty and skinny."

"Did your dad or his girlfriend get a good look at it? Did anybody call animal control?"

"I don't think so." Davy's voice ticked a notch higher. "Do you think it had rabies?"

"That's the hard part, honey. There's no way to know." Susan hadn't slept much last night, wrestling alone with near-terror in the wee hours. If the cat had rabies, J.J. was in horrific danger, but Matt hadn't seemed overly concerned, leaving her to decide whether she would take matters into her own hands. Of course, there was no question she would. Sometimes she felt like the only grownup in the family. Such as it was anymore.

Matt might feel she was sticking her nose where it didn't belong. Not like she cared what he thought, but she didn't want to lose contact again, like when he shut her out after Allie's death. He probably felt guilty about his new girlfriend, but it didn't matter. Susan had learned that grief made people do crazy things.

"Grandma, I'm thirsty."

"Here." She gave them sips from the water bottle.

The first time she lost Allie was right after Raymond was buried. Allie, then seventeen and an honor student, ran away from her dad's funeral. Susan tried every means to find her, without result. Six months passed; six months of moving like a zombie through her new widowhood, her grief, her life. And then one day, a text appeared on her phone.

Im fine. Stop freaking.

She responded to Allie's text with dozens of her own, to no avail. She tried calling the number, but nobody answered. Then, a week later:

W/ try 2 get away fr wk & CU.

Three weeks passed, three weeks of silence in response to Susan's messages.

And then:

U worry 2 much. Luv u 2.

When they finally saw each other again, a year later, Allie was riding behind a young man on a motorcycle, and she was pregnant with Davy. They moved in together; thank the Lord, it was in Susan's city, even if Matt lived on the ragged side of town. Allie was home.

Susan had saved the texts. They were all she had now - the texts, and her darling grandsons.

She twisted the top back on the bottle. She didn't have an actual plan in mind, except to somehow capture the cat and let the authorities decide. Beyond that, she didn't want to think.

She held J.J.'s hand as they continued walking down the rundown street. Old cars sat rusting in driveways. Broken fences bordered overgrown yards. She felt herself being watched. The neighborhood might be quiet, but every few houses or so, she glimpsed a neighbor turning back to her clothesline or garden. When that happened, Susan would yell, "Have you seen a scraggly black tomcat? With long hair?" No one spoke, answering only with a slow shake of the head or an unconcerned shrug.

They walked and walked. As Davy led her around the neighborhood, up one street and down another, she began to lose hope. They saw no yellow eyes burning from thirst, no foaming mouth, no ball of matted black fur hidden away in a dark corner. Susan began to think her mission was a waste of time, and she was stupid for doing it, but then the warm air would carry the fragrance of pepper trees or eucalyptus, or she'd notice the occasional working man's oasis in a shady backyard, and feel better somehow. The scruffy neighborhood was peaceful, and she was with her grandsons.

"Grandma." Davey raised his arm and pointed. "Look."

A big, dark cat lay sleeping under a bush. Susan approached quietly, to get a closer look, but J.J. saw the cat and screamed. He twisted and writhed against her grip, trying to get away. The cat streaked across the yard, squeezed through a hole in the fence, and disappeared.

Davy bolted across the yard and over the fence. Susan picked up J.J. and hurried around the far end, catching up with Davy on the next street. He was on all fours, straining to see into the black crawlspace under a ramshackle house.

"Don't go any closer," she said.

"But how are we going to get it out?"

"There's another way." They looked up, startled. A thin, young man stood above them on the porch, shirtless, his low-slung jeans exposing his boxers. "On the other side of the house." He turned to Davy. "I'll scare it back towards you. You got a box or somethin'?"

"We didn't think that far ahead." Susan flopped down in a stringy lawn chair on the man's porch and wiped a trickle of sweat from J.J.'s forehead. He looked over her shoulder.

"Hi, Daddy."

Matt strode toward them through the knee-deep weeds. With his long hair and beard, he looked like Charles Manson. She wasn't the only one who thought so. Allie used to joke about it, and the nurses at the chemo ward wondered, too, you could tell. But then after a few days they made up a bed for him, and after that, they brought him orange juice and toast every morning for breakfast.

And right now, he had a big, green net.

A loud clatter rang from the other side of the house, and a blur shot past Matt.

"What the–" He turned and raced after the cat, Davy on his heels.

"Get him, Dad!"

The young man leapt off the porch and joined the chase. Two neighbors appeared, holding rakes and brooms like hockey sticks. The cat ran the gauntlet, slinking through the tall grass and ducking behind lumber and rusting car parts, but the men turned it back again and again, tightening the circle, blocking its escape. When the cat sailed through the broken window of an old wooden shed, someone slammed the door.

Susan stood, slinging the little boy back up onto her hip. Her tired legs churned through the weeds toward the shed, now surrounded by tattooed boys and beer-bellied fathers.

A soft-spoken man gestured at the shed. "Is that the cat that bit 'im?"

Susan and J.J. peered through a broken window. "Honey, is that the cat that hurt you?"

He nodded. Then he tucked his head against her neck and began to whimper.

"I'll wait for Animal Control, if you want to go back to the house," said Matt.

Susan and Davy turned toward home, weighed down by a victory not worth celebrating.

"Grandma, what are they gonna do with the cat?"

She wondered how much he knew, and opted for a gentle version of the truth. "They'll have to watch it. If it's sick, J.J. might have to get a lot of shots."

They walked in silence for another block. Susan placed her hand on the back of Davy's neck. His skin felt as smooth as a toddler's.

A young woman with an infant leaned across a fence. "Didja get the cat?"

"I think so. I hope it's the right one."

"Big ol' black one with scraggly, long hair?"

Susan nodded.

"I hated that cat," said the woman. "It was real dangerous around kids."

Susan kept walking, rubbing J.J.'s small back as she carried him. The sun was getting lower, and at the house, somebody had chained up the dog and propped open the gates. They shuffled down the dusty driveway.

Setting the little boy on the porch, Susan kissed them both and turned to leave, her chest tight. She always hated leaving, feeling as though she was abandoning them to a lesser life. Today, though, the aroma of fried chicken wafted from the kitchen, arousing something resembling an appetite, if she could remember what that felt like. Susan heard the sound of a radio, tuned to a country station. A spoon clattered against a pan.

She touched Davy's shoulder, her eyes on the door. "Why don't you invite me in?"

~ 4 ~

THE GIRL FROM CIRCLE ISLAND

Ted unhooked the trout and held it in the current. Its notched tail waved feebly back and forth as it regained its senses, the same small fish he'd caught earlier.

"I don't understand why it keeps taking the lure," Julie said.

The trout jerked as if awakening and darted away into the shadows of the grasses hanging over the slow-moving stream. Ted stood up, his face expressionless. "Stupid or lazy, I guess."

"You'd think the pain would teach him to avoid it."

"You'd think." Ted clambered up the bank, fishing pole in one hand, tackle box in the other, his tee-shirt straining across beefy shoulders. Julie watched him move. Now in his sixties, he'd added layers of flesh like a bear bulking up for the winter. It wasn't fat, though. He was still narrow through the hips, and his thighs and calves were that of a forty-year-old. And oh, the arms – still the arms. How he used to hold her. But that was centuries ago.

Now, she scrambled after him, breathing hard, his fitness like a rebuke.

The next morning, Julie bungeed her lunchbox on the back of her bike and pedaled along the path to town. Wrens and thrashers, undaunted by the late-summer heat, warbled and trilled in the heavy limbs overhead. A young couple rode by on the other side of the slough, laughing and calling to each other, and Julie waved.

She ducked to avoid a veil of Spanish moss hanging overhead and coasted through the crowded parking lot at Circle Island Plaza, a half-dozen stores on Main Street. In the years she'd lived on the island, she had become a proficient bike rider. Locking the old Schwinn in the bike rack, she waited while a raucous family filed into the grocery store ahead of her. The parents debated a moment and then split off, the father toward the bakery and the mother, picnic supplies. The kids bounced in different directions, laughing and teasing each other.

"Hey." She greeted Carl, who watched the teenagers from behind the cash register, his eyes narrowing into a spangle of grimace lines. Most of her neighbors were crusty old salts, their skin scarred and tanned like ancient saddle bags. Beauty routines were considered exhaustive if one bothered to apply sunblock, and even that rarely occurred except after a midlife talking-to by the skin doctor. The island's one hair and nail salon survived on tourist traffic alone. Julie cut her own bangs, and if the rest of it got too wild, she pulled it into a ponytail or braids. Now in her mid-fifties, she was almost completely gray.

She grabbed an apron off a hook in the storeroom and began loading cases of bottled water onto a dolly. Ted hated the stuff; said it was an environmental disaster. Mostly it was tourists who bought it. They were a mixed blessing, bringing dollars to the island, but hard on it, too, leaving food wrappers and plastic grocery bags to blow onto the beach.

When she had loaded four cases, Julie rolled the dolly out the storeroom door and over to aisle fifteen. The end displays, messy from weekend customers, could be dangerous but were mostly unattractive. Julie set the dolly upright and lifted the first carton from the stack. She settled it on the shelf and repeated the procedure until the bottled water section was fully stocked.

"Morning, Doc." The voice belonged to Dave, the student worker. "What do you want me to do?"

"Stack the canned fruit on aisle five." Two kids ran yelling down the center aisle, and Julie thought of Ted. The tourists drove him absolutely ape-shit. By this point in the season, he'd begun driving around in the van, looking for scofflaws and writing down license numbers of those who'd parked illegally or fished in places that were protected. The local police dove for cover when they saw Ted coming, and he knew it, which only added to his irritation.

Her dolly empty, she turned for the stockroom but stopped short at the sound of glass crashing and breaking. A woman screamed, and Julie ran for the front of the store.

An adolescent boy lay on the floor in the midst of a collapsed display of wine glasses. His mother held his arm and babbled. Julie knelt down beside him. "I'm going to take a look, okay?"

When the boy nodded, Julie pried the mother's fingers away and studied the wound. It was deep enough he'd need stitches, but if she tied it off properly with a pressure bandage, he could get over to the mainland clinic without any problem.

Carl placed the first aid kit on the floor next to her. Julie cleaned the kid's arm with alcohol swabs, wrapped his wound with sterile bandages and surgical tape, and helped him to his feet.

"Keep an eye on his fingers," Julie told the mother. "If they start turning purple, loosen the bandage." Within minutes, the woman and her son were on their way.

Alice, the store manager, had watched silently. "We're lucky to have you."

"Don't mention it." Julie wadded up her bloodstained apron and returned to the stockroom for another load.

At noon she got her lunch from the refrigerator in the

employee lounge, unlocked her bike and pedaled north to the picnic area on the banks of the Intracoastal Waterway. After finishing the turkey sandwich, she reached into her backpack and checked her phone. Three new messages, not ten minutes apart, appeared on the display. Julie dialed the number.

"Are you coming?" Her twin's voice sounded more distant than before. Weaker.

"I haven't talked to Ted yet." Julie had avoided the subject entirely, knowing how upset he got when she updated him about her sister. He didn't trust doctors, seeming to have forgotten that Julie had been one, and she never brought it up.

"What are you waiting for?" asked Jeanette.

"I'm just –"

"They're stopping my chemo."

Julie groaned. "Why? What happened?"

"Nothing happened. My doctors can't do anything more, so I decided to enjoy myself. Hey, there's an upside: I can taste food again. When you come out, we can go to dinner, have some good times." Jeanette paused. "I miss you. I need you here."

"I miss you, too." Julie held the phone away from her face and swiped at her eyes. "I'll talk to him."

"Don't talk to him, Julie. Just leave."

Julie wanted to leave. Sometimes she wanted to leave small, like for a day or a weekend, just to get away from Ted's increasing moroseness. At other times, she wanted to leave big, say, a week at a hotel or a month at Jeanette's house in Charleston, to find her own rhythms again. And then there was leaving gigantic, as in forever. Moving to another state and leaving no forwarding address. But that would never work, because she herself would always be there. And from Julie there was no escape.

After work, she rode up the dirt driveway and leaned her bike against the garage. "You in there?"

"One second." The wooden door of the old structure opened, and Ted slipped out, blinking behind his steel-rimmed glasses like a mole exposed to sunlight.

Julie peered around behind him. "What's with all the canned food? Is that gasoline?"

"Empty cans. I'm recycling." Ted closed the door and clicked the padlock. He cleaned his glasses on the front of his shirt and put them back on. "What?"

"I'd like to ask you something." She led him to the picnic table under the maple tree where they had a view of the beach. A line of pelicans skimmed the waves, one trailing the other like smoke.

Ted sat on the table top and propped his feet on the bench.

"I need to go see Jeanette." Julie stood in front of him. "I've put it off too long."

"Thought you guys were doing fine with Skype."

"She's stopping chemotherapy. Her doctors said-"

"They don't know shit." He stroked his beard. For a long time he didn't say anything, and she tried to figure out what he was thinking. In the past, he would have tried to protect her with his cynicism, preparing her for the worst. Lately, it was more likely he'd be annoyed, thinking about the inconvenience of her leaving.

She attempted a conciliatory tone to camouflage her anger, both at him and at her acceptance of the role of supplicant. "I would like to go. Her life is so much harder now, and she needs help."

"Can't she hire somebody?"

"Ted, for God's sake."

"Don't get mad. Whether you go or not she should have help, right?"

She climbed up on the table beside him. "Sorry. I don't know what's wrong with me lately. Seems like everything's changing."

"Got that right." He looked away, off into the distance. "I need to tell you something, and I need you to not freak out, okay? That's really why I have the gas cans. It's backup, in case something happens."

"Do you mean like a hurricane or a power failure?"

"Way more than that, babe. The way this country is going..."
He didn't finish his sentence.

She'd heard it before, and nodded to reassure him. So what
if he wanted to stockpile supplies? "But still, I need to go see
Jeanette."

"What about your job?"

"Alice said I could use my vacation, and after that I could be
on unpaid leave."

"For how long?"

"Maybe a couple weeks is all. Just to make sure she has
help. Then I'll come home. After that, if things get worse, I'll go
back." He didn't answer. They sat for a long time like that, with
his arm around her, as the ocean turned rail grey and the sky
orange. When the mosquitoes started up, Julie slid off the table.
"I'm going to call and tell her I'm coming."

Ted climbed down off the tabletop and went back to the
garage.

Two days later, Julie arrived at the Charleston airport with
a small amount of baggage and a big headache. She saw a
uniformed driver holding up a sign with her name on it, and
followed him to a limousine parked out front. Through a lowered
window, her twin's thin white hand waved. Julie slid inside the
cool, dark interior and folded Jeanette into a long hug. Julie
could feel her twin's boney hips and ribs through her clothes,
and her skin felt cool even though the Charleston summer was
steaming. When the driver rolled the windows up, the glare and
noise of the city receded. As the limo glided through traffic
toward the historic Battery, Julie reached over and laid her hand
against her sister's cheek. Jeanette covered it with her own and
closed her eyes.

At Jeanette's house, a charming old waterfront bungalow,
they sat on the front porch and watched neighbors walk past,
their faces shaded by large hats and sun umbrellas. The house,
situated on a corner lot, occupied a knoll overlooking the blue

waters of the harbor, and in the far distance, the rusting artillery of Fort Sumter. Jeanette was bundled up in spite of the heat, a blanket wrapped around her legs.

"Sorry it took me so long to come out," said Julie.

"I'm surprised you're here at all."

"I have a job, too, so getting away isn't that easy. It's not just Ted." Julie picked up her glass of iced tea and studied the rivulets of condensation running down the sides. Not everyone understood Ted. Change made him uncomfortable, and he was turning into a curmudgeon, but he had a good heart. It wasn't that hard for Julie to make sacrifices for him; of the two of them, she was the stronger. Even Ted didn't know that.

On the street below, a horse-drawn carriage clopped by, on its way to downtown and hordes of tourists.

"Things aren't perfect," Julie said, "but I'm at peace."

"Are you?"

"Ted has his good side. Even though he's not working, he does all the domestic stuff. You should see our garden this year. Our yield has doubled. It's extraordinary." That was an understatement. Ted had traveled to the mainland to fill up his van with canning equipment.

"Listen to me." Jeanette leaned forward and grasped Julie's arm with cold fingertips. "Life's too short to be unhappy."

"I'm happy."

"Really. Is he working?"

"Not lately, but we're fine. We don't need that much." Julie felt her face getting hot. Why did she feel so defensive?

"Does he still hit you?"

"Come on, what is this? That was years ago. It was just that one time, and we were both drinking. I can't believe you even remember."

"You should have left him then. I wish you had left him."

"Well, I didn't. I decided to trust him, and I stuck around. And you know what? We're fine. We've been fine for years. You'll be happy to know we've turned into two boring old people with simple lives and no excitement. Everything is peaceful and mellow."

"So you're totally happy."

"Nobody's totally happy," said Julie.

Sighing, Jeanette stood up. "I'm exhausted."

After helping her sister prepare for a nap, Julie flopped in the guest bedroom and watched the blades of the ceiling fan spin around and around. And around.

She'd meant what she said. Life was boring and predictable with Ted. They were more like roommates now, and she figured that was due to their age. They rarely had sex anymore. In fact, they rarely did anything together anymore. And the older Ted got, the more paranoid he seemed. But all of it had happened gradually, and she'd adjusted. Wasn't that the wisdom of age – becoming more accepting of the bad? Acceptance was a survival skill. Jeanette should give her a medal instead of criticizing.

Julie fell asleep in spite of a throbbing headache.

She was awakened an hour later by the sound of the phone ringing, and Jeanette's laughter. "Burke, my neighbor down the street, invited us to have dinner with him so we wouldn't have to cook. I told him yes. He's a lot of fun; he knows the dirt on everybody in town."

"I didn't bring anything to wear, and my hair looks like crap." Julie tried to smooth it with her hands, but the humidity defeated her.

"Hmm." Jeanette appraised her and picked up the phone again. "I have a stylist who comes to the house. If that's okay with you?"

Three hours later, her hair newly colored and cut, and having found in Jeanette's closet an emerald silk dress that made the most of her cleavage and the least of her ass, Julie stepped into the living room for inspection.

Jeanette looked up from her magazine. "You look fantastic. Like your old self. Younger self, I mean. Who you used to be." She stood up for a closer look. "What do you think?"

Julie took her sister's hand. "I didn't think I could still look this good."

"I can't wait for you to meet Burke."

"Me neither, actually." Julie looked at her sister and they both giggled.

"We're bad."

"So bad," said Julie. "Let's go."

In a refreshing breeze off the ocean, they walked a block and a half to the neighbor's house, with Jeanette pointing out the history of the houses along the way. Burke was waiting for them on the steps. He surprised Julie by greeting her with a hug. "After all the stories your sister's told me, it's wonderful to meet you," he said. His deep voice was rich with South Carolina honey.

Julie leaned back, still in his arms. "What stories did she tell you?"

Jeanette walked in ahead of them. "Only that you're a world-class surgeon who chucked it all to go be a hippie in the Southern wild. That you raise all your own food. And you're married to an evil genius."

"One of those assertions is untrue," Julie said.

Burke let her go. "I'll try to guess later, but right now, I have to check my fire. You ladies help yourselves. Bar's over there, by the kitchen."

After a sumptuous meal of barbecued ribs with grits, greens and gravy, followed by pecan pie for dessert, Burke took Julie on an art tour through his sprawling antebellum three-story. On the second floor he had a gallery dedicated to artists who specialized in scenes of the Low Country.

"I can see why you're a fan," she said, admiring the sleepy southern landscapes.

"I'm a fan of anybody who can make a living at what he loves," said Burke. "This guy, for example. He travels up and down the coast in a fancy RV, stops when he feels inspired, and paints for as long as it takes. Then he goes home and sells his work."

"So he pays for his vacations with his art." Julie's breath quickened, but it wasn't about the lavish oils. Burke had reached for her hand and turned her until she faced him.

"I think I know which of the things your sister told me is untrue." He brought her hand to his lips as if to kiss it, but paused, as if breathing in her scent.

Julie could smell his aftershave, richening now with the warmth of his skin. "If you are correct, we are probably both in trouble."

He lifted his chin and laughed, and she wanted to reach up and trace his jaw. For a moment, she weakened. Then she reclaimed her hand. "We should go back."

He walked them home shortly thereafter, and after Jeanette had gone to bed and the house was dark, Julie poured a snifter of sherry and made her way out to her private veranda. There, she sat on a porch swing and listened to the sounds of a mixed-up mockingbird singing from a tree in the next yard. The neighborhood was quiet, leaving her free to consider the fact that she was as horny as a bitch in heat, and tired of going without.

In the morning, Jeanette came into the kitchen humming. "I thought I heard you up."

"Curious what was in the paper," Julie said, stirring another lump of sugar into her coffee.

"Uh huh. How'd you sleep?"

"Not great. I was restless. Probably too much wine," said Julie.

"Or something. He's a babe, isn't he?"

"He is that." Julie sighed.

The next evening, Burke took them to dinner at High Cotton, and the next, they cooked for him. By the fourth evening, Jeanette, professing exhaustion, begged off dinner.

Julie got home late. As she tried to sneak in quietly, so as not to wake Jeanette, she was dismayed to see the light on in her sister's bedroom.

"Jules? Can you come in here?"

Julie sighed. This night had been so amazing, she didn't want to spoil it by answering questions. She leaned against the door frame of her sister's room.

"This complicates things, doesn't it?" said Jeanette.

"Wasn't it supposed to?"

"You're your own person. You should decide for yourself."

"Do you mind if I turn in? I'm really tired." Julie turned and closed her bedroom door, grateful for the silence.

The next morning, she got up early and made a full breakfast for the two of them. Sitting at the sunny dinette in the bay window, she unfurled The Post and Courier, only half-interested. Last night had been wonderful. Burke had awakened in her a sense of gratitude for the finely working body she'd neglected. "Pure art," he'd said, running his hand over her slopes and contours. She shivered now, remembering.

Jeanette sat down across from her. "I remember you said you didn't wear a ring because of surgery."

"I never really said."

"You didn't have to. If you'd ever gotten married, I think I would have known about it," said Jeanette.

"I wanted to be married," said Julie. "I asked Ted more than once, but he didn't see the point. He saw it as the government interfering with what people should be able to do with their private lives. After a while, I stopped asking."

Jeanette stirred her coffee, took a slow sip, and set her cup down. "Last night, while you were with Burke, I called the kids. They agreed with my plan. We think you should forget about going back and stay here. The house is paid for. Live here as long as you want. Rent free. Start over."

Julie folded the paper and set it by her plate. Out the bay window, a tour boat churned across the harbor toward Fort Sumter. "You already discussed it with them?" She hadn't seen her niece and nephew in ten years, and yet they were concerned about her. That was not a surprise; they were good kids. It was also not a surprise that Jeanette made the offer. What surprised her was that Jeanette's idea awakened a sense of desire, so unfamiliar as to be unnerving. Besides, there was no reason not to. Ted would probably be happier alone in the house. Lately she'd just been getting in his way, and moving her things wouldn't be difficult. She had so little of her own.

"You still have your license to practice. I could get you a job like that." Jeanette tried to snap her fingers, but no sound emanated. "I know everybody at the hospital."

And yet it was premature. In spite of her pleasure with Burke, and Jeanette's generous offer, if she ever decided to leave, she'd want to tell Ted, and give him a chance to change her mind. Out of respect for their time together, plus it was only fair. "You're moving too fast. I never said I wanted to leave the island."

"How can you be happy? You've sacrificed so much. And what about when you get old? You'll never be able to retire."

"Work keeps you young." Julie poured fresh coffee into porcelain cups, using a silver teaspoon to stir in real cream. She laid the spoon on the saucer and considered the pattern. It was a pineapple, iconic sign of southern hospitality, braced on both sides by trailing ivy. The pineapple was made of gold. When she looked up, Jeanette was waiting.

Julie shrugged. "Living on the island is great. It's simple, not fancy. Nobody bothers you. They don't care what you look like. The pace suits me."

"I don't believe you."

"I've changed in my old age." Julie ran her fingers through her hair, feeling the expert cut, her hair both thicker and sleeker, as if that could be possible. In the hands of Jeanette's stylist it was not only possible but expected. Life in Charleston would be comfortable.

"Julie? Is it enough? For the rest of your life, is that how you want to live?"

Julie's hand dropped. "I don't know."

"God!" The word escaped Jeanette's lungs in a burst of

frustration. "You used to be so sure of yourself. Do you even remember who you were before you met him?"

"That life wasn't perfect either." Before Ted, Julie had reached her mid-thirties, loveless, childless, and trying to convince herself she was happy. One day, on impulse, she accepted a coworker's invitation to a party on Circle Island, just across the Intracoastal Waterway from the mainland. The party depressed her, and Julie left early. Giving in to a rare bout of self-pity, she drove down to the beach to watch the late afternoon sun turn the clouds pink and gold. A man helped a youngster net a fish from the surf, and when the man introduced himself, she felt grateful for the attention. Ted shared a bottle of wine with her, as well as the sea bass he caught and grilled. As the sky darkened, they lay on a blanket on the sand. He pointed out the constellations to her that night, and cooked her breakfast the next morning. Afterwards, she drove away, back to her job at the busy city hospital, to the clatter and crash of the ER where she worked graveyard and whatever else they needed.

Back then, Ted was employed part-time by the forest service, doing environmental surveys. On her days off, Julie rushed back to the island, her chest expanding with joy as she crossed the bridge, over yachts and ferries cutting wakes in the Intracoastal below. Back she rushed, to Ted and his quiet life.

Jeanette's voice cut into her memories. "You used to run marathons," she said. "Remember how skinny and tough you were?"

Julie nodded, her eyes downcast.

"You had money. You loved to travel." Jeanette was shaking, either from anger or cold. Julie helped her move to the living room sofa and covered her with a blanket. "Who is this man that he could throw such a spell on you?"

"He was in the right place at the right time."

"Is that it?"

Julie slipped into the wing chair next to Jeanette. "At the time, it was everything."

She and Ted had spent their days making love, reading, and strolling under the oak trees draped with moss. In the evenings, he would build a driftwood fire on the beach and grill the fish he'd caught. With the waves lapping at the shore, they drank wine and shared their histories until the fire burned low.

Back at work, with the allure of Circle Island always on her mind, Julie began to hate her job and her two-bedroom high-rise overlooking the city. Within months, she resigned from the hospital, sold her apartment and moved her belongings and her life to Ted's house on the island. The grocery store hired her as a cashier, and Ted continued working for the forest service until he got sideways with a supervisor and walked away. "We'll be fine," he said, and they were, for the most part, living in the house he'd inherited from his parents.

After a year, though, and bouts of stony silence, she learned to deal with his increasing irritation. He didn't appreciate her bringing people around, so she stopped. He grew reluctant to leave the island or to allow her to leave without complaining, so she stopped doing that, too. With each capitulation, her world shrank, but she adapted. At the time she assumed it was the power of maturity that allowed such adaptation.

Now she felt the leaden weight of bleak possibility: what if all she'd learned over the years was to rationalize her bad decisions?

"I don't understand," Jeanette asked, her voice hoarse.

"You get used to things. And to be fair, he has his strengths. He's brilliant. He can tell you anything about the stars, the earth, about chemistry and physics." Her voice trailed off. They sat quietly for a long time.

Julie broke the silence. "He's buying guns and stockpiling food."

Jeanette shivered.

"It sounds worse when I say it out loud," said Julie. "I mean, if you heard a TV reporter interviewing the neighbors saying the same thing after some terrible crime, you'd think they were idiots. I know that's what you're thinking, that I'm a fucking idiot. But I was used to his ways." As she talked, a giant moth fluttered up to the porch lamp, and they watched as it tried to decide whether to land on the hot surface. "Lately, I've been having nightmares. I wake up terrified, and he's not in bed. I get up and look for him, and he's always out in the garage."

"Doing what?"

"I'm afraid to go see. I don't want him to catch me snooping," Julie said. "It sounds crazy now, but I wanted something simple. Something authentic."

"That's not crazy," Jeanette said. "The rest is."

"The island is a small place. I felt safe there. God, I'm so stupid."

"Don't go back. Stay here. You can start over. If nothing else, do it for me."

Julie stared down at her lap, unsure of her own judgment. "I would like to stay here. I don't want to go back, but I don't know how to tell him."

"Say you need to stick around a few more weeks to help me. That'll keep him from getting suspicious. And there's somebody I want you to talk to, somebody I know at the hospital."

With Jeanette sitting next to her and holding her hand, Julie called Ted and broke the news. "It's what I expected," he said.

"It's only for a while. I'll come home as soon as Jeanette's stabilized."

He hung up.

Over the next two months, Julie saw Jeanette's therapist almost every day, and learned about codependency and post-traumatic stress disorder. Ted left her alone, and Julie wondered how he was doing without her. Occasionally, she called him, but their words were guarded and noncommittal. The therapist suggested Ted might not need Julie as much as the reverse, but Julie resisted. This was Ted's way of dealing with grief. Naturally, he would put up a front, trying to appear self-sufficient.

After a while, the distance between them began to make her feel anxious. She wished she could talk to him honestly, and explain that all she wanted was a little more autonomy, a little more material comfort. Maybe she could go back to work at the hospital part-time. She could earn her own money.

In spite of missing Circle Island, Julie was determined to press forward. She signed on with a personal trainer and worked out at Jeanette's athletic club. She told Burke she wanted to enjoy his friendship but that the relationship must remain platonic while she figured things out. She was contacted by a headhunter and promised to consider a job offer with the hospital, pending the outcome of her sister's illness.

As summer gave way to fall and Jeanette's health deteriorated, Julie took over her sister's care. From delivery of the hospital bed to administration of morphine, from making meals to cleaning house, she was happy to help. During a blustery week in October, she opened the house to friends and family who wanted to visit one last time.

In early November, Jeanette was moved to the hospital, and Julie moved with her, sleeping in the same room, on a roll-away bed. As her sister declined, Julie felt more and more alone. The hospital, bright and noisy at all hours, seemed the loneliest place on earth.

A week before Thanksgiving, she went back to Jeanette's house to meet with Ryan, Jeanette's son.

"This came for you." Ryan gestured toward a bouquet of lilies he'd trimmed and put in a crystal vase. Her heart pounding, Julie checked the florist's card, but the lilies were from Alice and her coworkers. Ted wasn't that kind of guy.

On Thanksgiving eve, Jeanette's heart gave out. Julie sat in the hospital room with her niece and nephew, lost in grief. Eventually, the tearful children stood and embraced her. "We're going back to the house," Ryan said. "Everybody will be coming by. See you in a little while?"

"Everything is arranged," said Julie.

The two kids left the room, the industrial beige curtains wafting in their wake. After they were gone, Julie sat in the hard plastic chair next to the bed and gazed at the contours of her beloved sister's face. She felt sure Jeanette would be proud of her. Never again would Julie fall into a rut of self-denial and sacrifice. She was wiser now. The amount of information she'd gathered, the things she'd learned about herself—that was Jeanette's gift, and Julie would always be grateful. Newly strong, with her confidence back, she knew her life would never be the same. She would never again be a victim.

Julie stood and crossed the room to the bureau. She pulled open the top drawer, sad fingers pushing aside the pajamas and robe, the hairbrush and face powder, looking for a memento, something symbolic of her twin, a trinket or item that she could take home that would mitigate Julie's grief and evoke Jeanette's spirit. Julie dug under the shirts and sweatpants, the bras and panties, until she found what would serve her purpose: an expensive bottle of face cream, the fragrance of which spoke of her sister. She held it in both hands against her heart, eyes closed, before slipping it into her purse.

She kissed Jeanette's cold cheek and walked through the front doors of the hospital. In the distance, the sun had set and the sky was turning purple with the approach of dusk. Julie clicked the remote, popped open the trunk and stowed the face cream inside one of her suitcases. Then she slammed it shut and headed south, back to her new life on Circle Island.

~ 5 ~

HIS LITTLE GAL

The sky – hard blue with cirrus clouds scraping across it – could only be found along the coast in early fall, just before the Santa Ana winds kicked in and covered everything with dust. Foolish old man, his late wife would have said, but that wouldn't begin to describe it. Suicidal, more like. Grady reached around and felt for his wallet. It was getting thin – the both of them were – but he'd fed it an hour ago when he closed his last account at the bank.

Now he parked the beat-up Ford F150 pickup – battered on the outside from a thousand construction sites, but immaculate inside the cab – down a side street, and hoofed it to the Montage. Years ago, he'd built the luxury hotel, an illusion of simplicity in the heart of money-crazed Laguna Beach. He held the door for a skyscraper blonde, who swept past without acknowledging the old man in the bomber jacket. She reminded him of Yvette, who he was meeting in a few minutes. He hoped she wouldn't keep him waiting too long this time. The place was expensive. He brushed at his wallet again. It was all he had.

Foolish old man.

Inside, the young hostess lit up when she saw him. "Grady! Where have you been?" He blushed when the girl, all cleavage and black linen, kissed him on both cheeks. He wondered why everybody did it now. Did they think they were in France? It seemed fussy, but on the other hand, a person would have to be stupid to complain about an extra kiss.

"We were worried," she said. "What have you been doing?"

"Layin' low."

She smiled. "Are you by yourself?"

"I'm expecting a young lady." Yvette was the granddaughter of a fellow rancher, back in Oklahoma where Grady originally hailed from. The rancher had called to give him a heads-up that the young woman was coming west and needed a job. Grady, flush at the time, hired her as a secretary at his booming construction firm. But that was a dozen years ago, and since then, she'd moved on, their fortunes veering in opposite directions. The last time he saw her, she was driving a Jag and sporting some fancy wristwatch looked to be worth a year's rent for most gals. Her track record was to go to work at a top corporation and cozy up to the boss. He thought she was selling herself short, but it wasn't for him to say.

The hostess took his hand and led him toward the bar like he was still a big shot, like she didn't know there was a recession going on, and builders like him were bitin' the dust. Well, that was fine. Soon enough they'd get a whiff of his money troubles and that'd put an end to all the double kisses and hand-holding.

The bar was set up to look like a cattle baron's library, everything faux-old ranch, the walls buttery yellow, the leather chairs and sofas a rich saddle-brown. Graceful silver and crystal chandeliers hung from the punched-tin ceiling. Except for the fact that the building was perched on a cliff over the Pacific Ocean, it could've been his place.

His former place. Bank owned it now. Grady sat down to wait, stub-nail hands gripping a double Scotch.

An hour later, there she was. Standing at the entrance to the bar, scanning the room until she spotted the old man. He waited at a table by the fireplace, faithful as a hound. Yvette adjusted her smile and strutted toward him in a slow version of the runway walk.

Grady rose to greet her, and Yvette doled out a hug as, throughout the room, hungry eyes coveted her luxurious frame. And that was just the women. "Sorry I'm late," she said. "Been runnin' errands. You know, pickin' up a few things for work." She settled into an overstuffed chair.

Grady noticed her speech pattern slipping into the old country rhythms. She talked a different way around other people, but with him, she must've felt like she could let down her guard. That made him happy. "Good as you look, you'll be running the company soon, I believe. What'll you have, darlin'? Apple martini, as usual?"

"Get me a Cosmo." Yvette surveyed the room. It was important to know who was there. Seeing no one to fear or flatter, she relaxed. "How are you? How are things at the office?"

"Just fine, doll." Grady shook his drink, working the ice cubes around in the Scotch. "Jimmy Earl says to tell you hi."

Yvette narrowed her eyes, and Grady remembered. How many times had she told him to stop bringing messages from Jimmy Earl?

"Listen to me, Grady. You tell that boy, next time he asks, that I said for him to take a flyin' leap."

Grady chuckled. "What's the problem, honey? He just misses you. We all do."

"The problem is, he's a dog."

"Most men are. You'll find that's true, sooner or later."

"But you're not."

"Probably because I'm too old."

"You're not old. You're seasoned. Women love that." She smiled, her mascaraed eyes turning into twin spiders. "So tell me about work. Any big jobs coming in?"

"Oh, yeah. All the time." Grady leaned back. The Scotch had hit bottom, creating a warm glow. "Everything is awesome. Isn't that what you kids call it?" He laughed, a deep rumble from forty years of unfiltered Camels. "Got a big-assed project startin' next month – we're going to scrape off an old mall in Tustin and put up some fancy new complex."

"Really? Because I heard that project got canceled." She frowned, her auburn brows knit over green eyes.

"Nah, just a couple delays. Then it will be full steam ahead as usual. You know me. Work, work, work." He signaled for another drink. Twenty bucks for a couple shots. There was a time it wouldn't have mattered. "How about you? How's the new job working out? Are you CEO yet?"

Her bee-stung lips formed a pretty pout. "No, and you won't believe what happened. My boss, the owner of the company? Really sweet man."

Her jaw tightened, and then Grady knew. He wasn't surprised; just disappointed, maybe. The waiter put another Scotch in front of him. "So, what's this about your boss?"

"The other night when it was raining? He was leaving a party and he crashed into a bridge. Died instantly."

She took a sip of her martini and wrinkled her nose, and he stopped breathing in spite of himself. He was a slave to redheads with freckles. Most gals in Orange County had them bleached away, but not Yvette. She even had her own boobs; at least, that's what he assumed from the looks of her. He turned away, confused. She could have been his daughter.

Yvette was still talking. Grady pretended to be interested in the dead boss man. "That's a shame. Did he have family?"

"No. Well, a wife, but they were gettin' divorced anyway." She gnawed off a cuticle and spat it out. "He told me his parents live in Palm Beach, Florida, right on the water. Richer than God."

"I'm sorry for them. It's hard to bury a child." He was surprised to see her upset. Usually she was pretty hardcore. Could be her age - she had to be heading down the southern slope of thirty by now. Or maybe she was starting to trust him, seeing as how he always came through when she had a problem. In the past couple years, their friendship had grown. Anyway, that's what he wanted to believe. "Don't fret, honey, you're gonna like the new owner just as much." He placed his hand over hers. She let it stay there, probably since the bar was half-empty and nobody important would notice.

"No, I won't. They already made the big announcement. His wife is taking over." Her drink was gone, and she eyed the waiter, but then turned back to her cuticle. "What a joke. She knows shit about the business. All she's ever done is be a housewife. I mean, God."

"How many kids?"

"Who cares?" She crossed her long, ivory legs to the appreciative stares of half the room.

Grady ducked his head, hurt by the comment but afraid to take it further. His late wife, Lorene, had always said looking after him and their four boys was more work than digging ditches all day long. How she would laugh if she could see him now.

"I never worked for a woman boss who wasn't paranoid, insecure and power-crazy," said Yvette. "They always have these - issues. And they expect you to be their best friend and their shrink, but then the minute you do something wrong, look out. They'll throw you out like last week's trash."

"Must be tough."

Yvette heaved a big sigh. "I don't even know if I'm going to have a job come Friday."

"Now, honey, don't you worry. You'll land on your feet, just like you always do."

"But there's talk of layoffs."

"Nobody would let you go, sweetie. They wouldn't be that stupid."

"I don't know. I never get any credit. It's like they think customer service is easy."

"Customer service? I thought you were in the executive suite."

"Not anymore." She shook her head. "I swear, some days I go home so depressed."

He leaned sideways, reached into a back pocket, and extracted his wallet. "Here, let me float you a bit a' capital to tide you over – no, don't argue with me," he said firmly over her tiny protestations.

Yvette grabbed the several hundred dollars he'd laid on the table and stuffed them in her purse. She jumped up and flung her arms around his neck. "Grady, you're such a sweetheart. I don't know what I'd do without you."

He reached up and patted her arm. His eyes closed. Her perfume filled his nostrils.

Yvette glanced at her watch, a diamond-studded Tank Francaise. "My God, look at the time. I'll be late for my job on the suicide hotline." She grabbed her jacket from the bemused waiter and raced out the door.

Grady watched her go.

"Still working on that drink?" The waitress' teeth flashed such a brilliant shade of white they almost looked blue.

"I'm finished," Grady said. At the doorway, he ignored the eager approach of the valet, and turned left down the sidewalk toward self-parking.

~ 6 ~

HER ALBIE

I don't want to do this.

First, I have to find some clothes to sacrifice, like sweats, sneakers, and shorts that can get good and bloody. Next, I need a hat, sun block and medication. And a book. Definitely a book. Something good I can hide behind, assuming quarters are cramped and I'll need mental privacy, or that I'll be bored out of my skull and need something to help me kill time. This pretty much summarizes my low expectations for the three-day fishing trip I have agreed to take off the coast of San Diego. I'll be accompanying my husband and two teenaged sons.

Nothing about this trip makes sense, because I do not fish, and I get seasick. For me to step aboard an ocean-going vessel, it has to be at least the length of several football fields. Preferably with hot tubs, pools, and bar service.

I drag myself to Wal-Mart for a fishing license, come home, resist packing until the last minute and then resign myself to it. Half-hour later, I'm done. One medium canvas bag.

"You're a champ" says Bill. He's just happy not to have to

bunk with a stranger, since his buddy cancelled at the last minute. To hear Bill tell it, the boat is like a cruise ship without a pool. "The water's glass and the fish are committing suicide," he tells me. This is what he always says. However, we both know the minute I set foot onboard, things will change. The water will become tumultuous, and the fish will stop biting.

When we arrive at the wharf in San Diego, the boat isn't ready for boarding, so we have lunch outdoors at Hudson Bay Seafood. Commercial fishing boats bob in their slips, waiting. Soft white clouds dot a pure blue sky. My sons, Jeff and Dan, wolf a half-dozen tacos and then pace up and down the boardwalk, impatient.

Finally, we get the go-ahead to come aboard and load our gear into a wheeled cart. The boys haul it down the ramp toward the dock where the Polaris Supreme is tied. The boat, in my opinion, is small. The passengers, except for me, are all men.

The boys are excited. "I'm glad you're here, Mom," says Dan. He even lets me hug him, and I act like it's no big deal. Secretly I could weep. He's in his late teens now, so I don't get to hug him very much anymore.

The boat is relatively spacious. There are four heads – two with showers – and as I cast a suspicious eye about, I'm relieved to see that they are pristine. The room I'll be sharing with Bill consists of a bunk bed, a sink and a closet. It's dark but well-ventilated and looks comfortable. If nothing else, I can lie in my bunk and read by flashlight.

After unpacking we're called into the galley for an announcement. Captain Vic growls out a pre-trip orientation regarding everything from life rafts to what to do when we get a fish on. He tells us to holler loudly so he knows to cut the motors. "Otherwise, I can't hear you over my radio and equipment," he says. The fishermen nod, their faces solemn.

As the boat pulls away from the dock it begins to hop around a bit, but the medicine's kicking in, so I don't feel queasy. We motor through the harbor and pull up at the bait dock, a floating barge where the fishermen buy small fish with which they hope to catch bigger fish. A harbor seal lurks near the dock, trying to come aboard for a snack, but the handler takes his stance, shovel resting on shoulder like he's aiming for the fences. The seal gets the hint and slips beneath the surface.

After we leave the bait dock, Bill shows me to a deck up above where there's a cushioned seat and a good vantage point. We pass the Hotel del Coronado, as well as numerous sail and power boats and one aircraft carrier. A few minutes later we're out of the harbor. Bill tires of babysitting and goes back downstairs to organize his tackle, so I investigate the boat. Near the bow I open a door and stumble across the threshold into the wheelhouse where Captain Vic is nice enough to show me around the bridge. His satellite-linked computer can identify significant changes in water temperature, called rifts, where fish come to feed. He steers an old-fashioned nautical wheel and tells me he's never out of touch with land.

The afternoon lull sets in as the boat motors toward Mexico. Deckhands drop jig lines off the stern. The men will be trolling in five teams of four each.

Just north of Baja, a dozen fishermen holler "Hook up!" They bellow deeply, in enthusiastic compliance with the captain's instructions. Vic cuts the motors. I watch in fascination as the men perform the Under-Over Dance, wherein the guy with the hookup has to walk around the boat following the fish and reeling. This is complicated by the presence of the rest of the fishermen who are all baiting up and dropping lines at once. They need to get out of each other's way or the lines will get tangled, and if they do it wrong, someone will get hurt.

"Under!" the fisherman cries, slipping under somebody's rod. "Over!" and somebody ducks under his. If you don't let him get around you with his rod, your lines can cross and one will saw the other in half. If you cause a problem, a deckhand will stick out his knife and cut your line. Goodbye tackle and self-respect.

I wonder how do these men know what to do and how will I learn everything in time for my turn at the rail? The seas are a little choppier now, so I practice my footing. The deckhands – Gringo, Chris, Don and Kevin – watch over everybody like sun-scorched angels. When a fish is caught, they'll gaff it and haul it over the rail, while hollering instructions and keeping people from getting stabbed or knocked overboard.

Nervous and slightly nauseated, I feel like an alien, differentiated from the rest of the passengers not just by gender but by what I now understand is a vast body of essential knowledge they have and I lack. We have nothing in common, and I am in the way. I go below and crawl into my bunk because there's nowhere else to sit in the cabin. It's too dim to read and the rocking boat lulls me to sleep. An hour later I'm awakened by the captain over the PA. He is directing Team Two to take over trolling. I don't know who Team Two is, but I figure I should go up and take a look just in case. Sleepy and off balance, it's all I can do to stay upright. Up on deck, I see a sturdy post, wrap my arms around it and look for Bill. He's at the stern, waving me over, and I realize Team Two is us.

Bill gestures to grab my fishing belt and be ready. I stagger to the rail, clip on the belt, and practice balancing and leaning, trying to act like I'm not scared. I rehearse mentally: if I get a fish on, I'll grab the fishing pole, jam it into the holder on my belt, keep the pole up as the boat rises on the waves, then crank quickly as we come down. Lather, rinse, repeat.

Rrrreeeeeee!!! A line sings. Regrettably, it is attached to the pole assigned to me.

"Hookup!!!" Twenty eager men scream with joy. We're into serious albacore tuna. Bill grabs the pole and puts it into my hands. His arm encircles me and now I'm cranking and pumping, walking along the rail as Bill yells, "Under! Over!" Frenzied men obey. I obey, too. My job is to wind and keep dancing in the direction set by the fish and Bill.

Something is wrong. I can't get air. I'm hyperventilating. I sound like a barking seal.

"Breathe!" yells Chris. "Keep winding, keep winding!" I hold the pole straight at 11:00. As the boat dips down, I reel, and as it comes back up I hold it steady, letting the boat do the work. Minutes later my arms are so tired I can barely turn the crank. All that time at the gym and for what? My muscles are mere anchors for the work of the boat, as I can no longer wind. Chris stays with me as Bill has gone somewhere else to fish because they are committing suicide.

Suddenly Gringo leans over the rail, sinks the gaff and pulls up a fat and feisty twenty-one pound albie. I'm excited but so tired I can barely smile. My arms hang limply at my sides. Jeff, Dan, and Bill beam at the other fishermen. They are proud of me.

After we take a picture I reattach myself to the post, but I am happy. The first fish of our trip was mine, and I am warmed by the congratulations from my fellow fishermen.

The next time the trolling poles sing, Bill and the boys are all fighting fish at the same time. It's a bloodbath, and I'm so excited that I pull out my camera but Kevin yells to put it away. He dashes to the rail to gaff a big tuna. When a bite is on, you've got large hooks, sharp knives, a bloody, slippery deck and a rolling boat, not to mention the fishermen elbowing each other to keep their lines working. It's not a good Kodak moment.

I see my sons' biceps bulging and the life-and-death grimaces on their faces, and I begin to realize what this trip means to them. They are happy here, using every bit of their muscle and wits against a wild animal who doesn't want to be eaten. When they're on land, they must pine for this bloody battle.

Who are these boys? While I wasn't looking, they turned into men.

When the bite ends, Captain Vic comes on the PA and directs us to pull in our lines because we're moving out, in search of more hot spots. Lethargy settles over us. Our legs are splattered with blood, and our arms are limp and shaky, but we all caught a fish. As the sun lowers inside Mexican waters, we get into bite after bite. The tuna are hauled on board, filleted on the spot, and tagged for later retrieval. The freezer holds twelve *big* albacore. A third of them are ours. I high-five my sons, wanting to hug them but sensing we're moving forward into a new place now. Still, I can't keep from grinning with pride. My men know how to hunt.

At dusk the communal dinner is ready, but the seas have come up, and I can't eat. Half my fellow fishermen are slightly green as well. Whose idea was it to serve Clams Alfredo? Two small bites and I'm down for the night.

The next morning, Bill showers and shaves by five a.m., but the rest of the boat is still asleep, so he goes back to bed fully dressed and ready. I smile into my pillow at his eagerness. At 5:40, Captain Vic's voice comes softly over the PA, "Good morning, it's time to get up. Good morning, fishermen, good morning. (Pause.) LET'S DO SOME FISHING!" Bill is out the door and up the stairwell before the Captain is finished.

I stay in bed a little longer. I suspect it's cold and overcast outside, and the boat is pitching and rolling, so the decks will be more dangerous than usual. An hour later, I hear shouting, and Captain Vic comes on the PA. We're into bluefin, a prized tuna we hadn't expected to see on this trip. This fish can reach two hundred pounds, so Vic orders the men with lighter lines to reel them in so the guys with proper rigs can do their job.

No doubt there is drama overhead, irreplaceable moments in the lives of my husband and sons. Happening right now, above-decks on a miserable sea. Will I choose the safe route, remain snug in my bunk, and miss it?

No way. I dress quickly, pop another Dramamine, and ricochet from wall to wall on my way topside. Just as I straggle out on deck, Bill hooks a monster. He's one of only three fishermen to hook up, and in spite of the Captain's orders, Bill has caught it on anemic 25-lb. test, with a little pole that's gone all bendo. To further complicate matters, Bill missed a guide hole when he threaded the line onto his pole this morning. Captain Vic clears the decks, and I cross my fingers as Bill battles the tuna. Minutes pass and we all watch, suffering with him as he walks the line around the boat, sweat pouring off him. Finally, he reaches a point where he cannot fight any longer. He surrenders the pole to young Kevin, who soon lands sixty-four pounds of flopping, angry tuna. I dance across the deck, peck Bill on the lips, and scurry back to safety. This catch was my husband's opus, and I'm glad to have challenged myself to come out of my nest and bear witness.

We rest a while in the galley. The Dramamine isn't working so I go below to sleep a few more hours. Somehow being horizontal defeats the seasickness, at least until I stand again. But I can't sleep forever, and I'm getting cabin fever. Above deck, the sun is out, and patchy clouds keep it cool. The fishermen spot whales and visit with each other. It's pretty clear things have slowed down. We may have had our last good bite of the weekend.

Just before lunch, Jeff brings in a respectable sized albacore, and I am happy for him. After a hearty meal of burgers and potato salad, we flop on the couches and drape over chairs, somnolent and reptilian while Captain Vic motors to a place he thinks will be productive. I pull out my book, shy in the presence of all these men. Conversation is minimal. This is what a lot of fishing is, Bill says. Napping or quietly talking while waiting for the line to sing. Eventually the motors go silent. A fisherman snores. The boat rocks gently, and I read my book, content in literary solitude.

"Hook up!"

Jeff comes straight off the floor from a dead sleep, his legs churning, eyes glazed. Were it not for my warning shout, he would have steamrolled a wispy Asian grandfather on his way to the rail. Fishermen spill out onto the deck as if fire has been declared. Someone has hooked an albacore. The man hauls it up and we keep trolling. The bite goes on and the afternoon is fine.

My menfolk are happy. Soon the hold is full. Dinner is festive. Some have brought wine, and they share. The fishermen brag and hail one another.

The next morning we head for home. As grateful as I am to have lived in their world for three days, and to have seen what they treasure and why, I am thrilled that it will soon be over. Proud that I was a good sport, I still know that I will never again step foot on a fishing boat, because for all the positives, I finally found my limit. My love for my husband and boys – but they're not boys anymore, I realize again with a stabbing pain in my heart – will not compel me on another such excursion. This certainty makes me feel both safer and a little sad. The nausea begins again, but I take a few breaths and it disappears. As we motor north toward San Diego, I lose myself in *Bad Dirt* by Annie Proulx.

"Must be a good book."

I look up, guilty. "Yes, it is."

The fisherman nods. He turns and shuffles toward the fantail.

~ 7 ~

BARELY AFLOAT

A long line of passengers, many of them elderly, waited outside the cruise terminal. Lacking chairs, they stood wobbling on artificial knees and replacement hips, sweltering in the unexpected San Francisco sunshine. Their hats and sun block were already stowed in luggage that had been hauled away earlier.

Nancy, fifteen years younger but feeling newly sympathetic, flagged down a burgundy-jacketed member of the ground crew. As the young woman approached, she ran her hand through her hair, front to back, and then shook it. Nancy thought the gesture looked like she was advertising, but the effort was wasted on this crowd.

"Can I help you?" asked the youngster.

"Those older people are suffering," Nancy said. "Can't you at least put out some benches?"

"We don't have any."

"Well, then, how long before we can board?"

"They haven't told us." The girl shrugged. "The ship just got back from thirty-one days in South America, so that could be why it's taking longer."

"Well, thank you so much."

"No problem!"

"That was pointless." Nancy sat next to her husband, Chuck. She felt annoyed at the girl and guilty about the elderly people, because while they baked outside, she and Chuck got to wait in an air conditioned building. They'd paid extra for the privilege in celebration of the reason for the cruise: Nancy's enforced retirement, which she was trying to see as a chance for reinvention. But as she watched the slender young woman walk away, swishing her glorious long hair, Nancy felt old.

While they waited, rumors circulated. Some passengers said the reason for the delay was the discovery of smuggled drugs. Others said it was because of a stowaway; still others, a death. Nancy suspected incompetence. The cruise industry was lately besieged by problems. One ship ran aground off the Italian coast, killing thirty-two passengers. Another had to be towed in from the Gulf of Mexico, reeking from a week of unflushed toilets and mounds of garbage. This particular cruise line had been problem-free so far.

An hour later, a commotion ensued. The officials had opened the loading bridge from the terminal to the ship, and the crowd surged forward. Less than five minutes later, the ground crew again closed the bridge.

"What the hell?" said Chuck, as the crowd fell back, complaining.

"Too many people boarding at once," said a passenger. "They're afraid it'll collapse."

Nancy, picturing soft bodies tumbling to the pavement below, wondered if this cruise was a mistake, but eventually they boarded the ship without incident. After finding their stateroom, she followed Chuck as he marched from dining room to dining room, trying to confirm their seating reservations, which had gone missing. After receiving a series of hollow reassurances and making a last-ditch plea at the passenger services desk, Chuck and Nancy gave up. For the moment, they were resigned to dinner at the buffet.

At 9:30 that night, their suitcases landed outside their door with a thump. Chuck opened the door to the sound of an irate passenger haranguing the steward over the size of her small closet. The steward, his voice low, tried to placate the woman. A door slammed, and the muffled sound of yelling could be heard next door.

Too tired to unpack, Chuck and Nancy fell into bed, exhausted.

At 11 p.m., Nancy awoke to the sound of gurgling. Chuck was in the bathroom, where the sound originated. "Are you all right?" she asked.

He stuck his head out of the bathroom. "It's not me. There's something wrong with the shower drain. The sound woke me up."

The guttural burbling continued.

"Are the pipes backing up?" Nancy clutched the sheet to her chin. She had a phobia about unruly plumbing.

"Not yet. Maybe it's just noise, but it smells rank in there. Did you notice?"

"I figured it was mildew," she said. "The shower curtain is a little moldy."

"Nothing we can do until morning, but just in case something happens, I put our suitcases on top of the desk." Chuck slid under the covers. "Good night."

Nancy jammed in a couple of earplugs and went back to sleep, where she had nightmares about sewage.

In the morning, they found a letter from the dining room manager in their mailbox. Over lukewarm coffee at the buffet restaurant, they read the letter, which contained profuse apologies and reassurances that their dining-room reservation had been restored.

Nancy looked up from the letter to see a crowd had formed

near the coffee station. The crowd parted in deference to a teenager wearing the uniform of a ship's captain. "No way," she said.

"Is that him?" asked Chuck. The teenager approached their table.

"Good morning," the kid said, beaming at Nancy and Chuck. His hair was parted on one side and slicked down with gel, and his dress whites were impeccable. His voice wasn't much deeper than a girl's. "I wish you a magnificent day." The captain bowed slightly and moved on. Nancy began to choke on a desiccated pastry. Chuck jumped up to pound on her back.

"I'm fine," she said, gulping cold coffee. "But God help us."

Returning to their stateroom, they saw their steward out in the hall pushing his cleaning cart, and asked about the gurgling sound. It seemed pronounced when they ran the tap or flushed the toilet.

"It is the motion of the ship, ma'am," said the steward.

"I've been on a lot of cruises and never heard it before," Nancy said.

The steward nodded. "Yes, but it is an old ship, ma'am. Have a nice day." Armed with toilet paper, he ducked inside the stateroom next door.

Back in their room, Nancy pushed the drapes apart, tearing her finger open on an exposed curtain hook.

Chuck handed her a washcloth to staunch the bleeding. "That's pretty bad. You might need stitches."

"The heck with that. I'm not spending all day in the infirmary." She sat on the bed. "Help me put on a bandage. I have to cancel my appointment at the spa."

"Why not just call?"

"I need to walk off some calories." Nancy climbed the stairs to the spa deck. "I'm here about my manicure," she said. The young man looked up. His skin was so smooth it was either proof of the efficacy of their facials or the fact that he had not yet begun to shave.

"Yes, ma'am. When would you like to be seen?"

"I'm here to cancel my appointment."

"Your name?" When she told him, he frowned at the computer screen. "I don't seem to have you down."

"It's for two-thirty. I set it up online, weeks ago." She pushed the printed confirmation across the counter toward him.

He glanced at it. "We don't always get those." He typed something on the keyboard. "Perfect. We have you down, then."

"No, what I'm here for is to *cancel*." She held up the bandage. "I can't get a manicure because I tore my finger open on one of your drapery hooks."

"Ah." The young man nodded. "Yes. So sorry. But perhaps now you have time for a facial? Or a pedicure? We have a special rate –"

Back at her stateroom, Nancy found that the Passenger Services Desk had left a voicemail on the phone. "I'm sorry, but there is simply no way we can accommodate you in the dining room," the message said. "If you would like to discuss it further, you may do so in person; however, I assure you we have we have no alternatives available." The man repeated the message twice.

Nancy deleted it. "He must not have heard that they already solved the problem."

"They're pretty disorganized," Chuck said.

That night they located their table in the dining room.

"Good evening, ma'am. Good evening, sir." The waiter pulled out a chair and draped a napkin in Nancy's lap. Overhead, she noticed three strips of heavy industrial tape holding up a stretch of decorative moulding on the ceiling. "I think that's a first," she said to Chuck.

Regardless, the meal was delicious and the service excellent. After dinner, they watched the cabaret show, which featured half-naked women dancing around on the stage. Chuck took Nancy's hand. "Maybe we should go back to the stateroom," he said, halfway through the performance.

Equally inspired by the show, Nancy agreed. They

undressed each other and climbed in bed. Who's old now, she thought, smiling into the darkness as Chuck got her going. It had been a while, what with her depression over losing her job, and his parents both dying in the past year, and imminent dementia beginning to surface in her best friend. Life was too tough and scary not to enjoy the beauty when it was offered. Putting all that out of her mind, she arched her back, feeling the first flickers of the warm flame that would bring her to ecstasy.

The phone rang.

"Oh, my God," said Nancy, imagining the worst as tore herself away from Chuck and reached for the phone. "Hello?"

"This is the Passenger Services Desk. I'm calling in regard to your dinner reservations."

"Yes, they're fine. Thank you for calling." Nancy began to hang up.

"We've left a number of messages, none of which you've returned. I'm calling in this regard, ma'am."

"What messages?"

"We have left numerous messages, asking you to call us back in regard to your dining request. We have been working to find a solution and were waiting to hear from you."

Nancy's brain began to clear. "Do you realize it's eleven at night?"

"Did I wake you?" He sounded almost hopeful.

"Yes, I was asleep." What else could she say? "I'm hanging up now. Please don't call again."

"What the heck was that all about?" Chuck asked.

"He was calling late on purpose."

"What a jerk." He raised the sheet. "Come back here."

Nancy did, but she couldn't get the man out of her head. He'd sounded young and exasperated.

In the morning she dressed, put on makeup, and went to the Desk. Letting others go ahead of her, she waited for one of the clerks, the only male behind the counter. When he called on her, she recognized the voice. Showing him the letter confirming their dining reservations, she smiled respectfully, acknowledging her part in any miscommunication and offering her sincere apologies. The young man was trapped. He blushed and apologized as well. They shook hands over the counter.

Chuck gave her a thumbs-up as she related the story.

He wasn't a bad guy. Just frustrated. But this boat – I wonder. It almost doesn't seem safe."

"I read in today's newsletter that it's the oldest in the fleet, but ships last forever if they're well maintained. Hey, how about we go upstairs and soak in the hot tub?"

"I should give this one more day," Nancy said, holding up her bandaged finger. "I think I'll stay here and send out résumés." She settled into a chair and opened her laptop.

The next morning, they wandered around the Atrium. The stores were open and she went in, looking for toothpaste.

"We're all out, ma'am," said the clerk.

"But we just left port two days ago."

"It's down below, still waiting to be unpacked," said the clerk.

"Well, can you show me to the antibiotic hand cleaner?"

"We don't stock it, ma'am. Would you like some hand lotion?"

"Is that how you wash your hands?" It was rude, but Nancy couldn't help herself.

The clerk smiled. "If that's all there is, ma'am."

Chuck was waiting for her outside the shop. "I noticed in the men's room, a lot of the sinks aren't working."

"I saw that in the ladies', too. I wonder if they just put up 'out of order' signs to cut down on the need to clean."

"Worse. I asked the attendant, and he said they were out of sensor batteries, the ones that make the water come on when you put your hands under the faucet."

"Something as simple as that, they can't even keep up with? Makes you wonder about how well they maintain their food and water systems." Nancy pulled her camera out of her purse. "I'm going to start taking pictures. If we end up sick, I want evidence."

"Good idea."

They donned swim suits after lunch and went upstairs to the hot tub. The sun was out, the water in the Jacuzzi was clear and hot, and the seas were smooth. Later, they went down one deck to the outdoor pool, ordered tropical drinks and prepared to read for a couple hours.

A cry of pain interrupted them. A passenger had walked under a stairway, smacking his forehead on the low beam. "They should have a barrier around that," said Nancy. "A potted plant, at least."

The woman lying on the next lounge said, "Or maybe the old dude should watch where he's going." She smiled at Nancy, her brilliant laminates reflecting the sun. "I'm Madison, and this is my husband, Jason."

Nancy introduced herself and Chuck. "We've been noticing the disrepair and lack of maintenance all over the ship."

"Now that you mention it," Madison said, "we were at the nightclub last night and the comedian tripped over an electric cable. It was funny. We thought it was part of the show."

"Have you met the captain?" asked Nancy. "He's very young for a ship this big." Counting passengers and crew, the captain presided over a small city of nearly six thousand.

"He's my age," Jason said. "Thirty-eight."

"He's probably just really good," said Madison.

Nancy made a face. "Or maybe the pay's so low, they couldn't find anybody with experience. The reason the boat's such a mess is he's too young to command respect and whip it into shape."

"Well, I don't know about that," said Madison. "But you're right, the ship is old, so we can't expect as much."

The two couples went back to their reading. A while later, Chuck and Nancy returned to their room. Chuck napped while Nancy sat at the desk with the slider open, working on her computer. She liked the sound of the ocean sshhushing by the hull. It was peaceful – just what she had dreamed of. The other two things she desired were to have a cocktail with Chuck in the romantic nautical bar, and to sit for hours on the promenade deck. She would watch the seas rush by, and plan the rest of her life.

Such as it was. She closed the computer and stared out to sea.

On her way to the gym the next morning, Nancy took pictures of rusting and corroded metal, peeling paint, carpet coming up from the floor and other examples of overdue maintenance.

After lunch, she and Chuck went back to their stateroom and read on the balcony. The ship had reached the middle of the Pacific, in water a thousand feet deep and hundreds of miles from land in any direction. Chuck was immersed in the latest Prey book while Nancy kept rereading the same opening sentences of hers. She couldn't stop thinking about her young ex-boss, and their last meeting. He had called her into his office and announced that in future, she would be telecommuting instead of reporting to work each day. Assignments would be emailed to her as they arose, which they did with less and less frequency. After a while, there were no more assignments. Very slick, the way she'd been eased out of a lifelong career.

She watched the ocean go by. Unemployed, at sixty-three years old. What was she supposed to do now? Who would hire her? And even if she found something, it wouldn't last. She'd be working for young people and the same thing would happen all over again.

"Don't worry. Something will come up," Chuck had said earlier, giving her a nice long hug. "You're smart, you're up to date, and you look good."

She shook her head. "I'm an old tub."

Chuck borrowed her laptop to check his email. After a few minutes he handed the computer back. "I can't get online. Is the Internet down?"

"It was fine this morning."

"It isn't now."

She fiddled with it, but Chuck was right.

The next day, it still wasn't working. When she called the Passenger Services Desk, the clerk said they were urgently working to restore service as quickly as possible.

"Could be we're out of satellite range," Chuck said.

"How can that be? They need communication with a satellite to run the ship's navigational systems." Nancy eyed her computer. The fact that she couldn't look for a job now seemed the least of her worries.

They ordered a pizza from room service for dinner. Inexplicably, two pizzas were delivered. The pepperoni was good. They finished that. Nancy thought she'd have one small piece of the second one, a decision she quickly reversed upon discovering it was the special pizza of the day – the one they had deliberately not ordered.

"Who the hell eats tuna pizza?" she said. "It stinks to high heaven."

Chuck set the box near the stateroom door. "At least we can't smell the bathroom drain anymore."

The next night, the Internet still down, Nancy said, "I think I should call home and check our messages, even though it's horrendously expensive. I mean, what if there's been an emergency and they're trying to reach us?"

Chuck sniffled and blew his nose. "I think I have a cold."

She dialed several times, but the call kept reverting to a busy signal. Frustrated, she called the desk.

"Yes, ma'am, the Internet is currently out of service, ma'am."

"But I'm trying to use the phone."

"It's all connected," the woman said. "When one goes down, it all goes down."

"How long do you expect this to last?"

"Our technicians are working on it as we speak, ma'am."

"So we have no phone and no Internet."

"Yes, ma'am."

Nancy hung up. "Everything's dead."

"They'll get it fixed."

"But what if something happens? What if we all get sick? What if the crew mutinies? How would we contact land?" She began to feel a scratch in the back of her throat. "We're on a ghost ship."

After a fitful night, they arrived the next morning at their first port, Hilo, three hours late. They went ashore with just enough time to grab a hamburger in town before having to head back to the docks.

At the second port, Honolulu, Nancy awoke with a cold. They spent the day sightseeing, after which Nancy's handbag was filled with wadded up Kleenex. That evening, at the romantic Royal Hawaiian on Waikiki Beach, she watched Chuck, who had recovered from his cold, consume a forty-dollar entrée while she, lacking any appetite or sense of smell, contented herself with a cup of hot tea.

At their third port, Kauai, transportation away from the dock was limited to free shuttles sponsored by stores hoping to pull in the tourists. While the Kmart shuttle sat empty and waiting, Nancy and Chuck crammed aboard the shuttle destined for Duke's on the Beach. The driver packed them in until it was standing room only, and then took off, lurching across the pocked blacktop.

"Aren't we supposed to have seat belts?" Nancy asked the driver.

"We're safe, ma'am. Certified by the cruise line."

Nancy sat back and gripped the armrests more tightly.

In Maui, the fourth and last port, the plan was to tender the passengers ashore. When Chuck and Nancy arrived on time at the designated lounge to pick up their tickets for departure, the staff was still setting up. After receiving his ticket, Chuck asked what deck they'd be disembarking at. The ticket lady didn't know, but she waved toward the Atrium. "Sit in there so you can hear the announcement," she said.

"How can they not know?" Nancy whispered to Chuck. Just then, a large crowd of passengers spilled from the elevators and galloped toward the ticket tables. Chuck grabbed Nancy's hand and pulled her out of the way, toward the staircase.

"They'll have to go downstairs," he said. "We need to beat the crowd."

They passed a maintenance worker carrying a bucket. "Would you happen to know which floor we'll be getting off at?" Nancy asked.

"Deck Five," the man said.

Downstairs, they found a tender waiting and climbed aboard. After a choppy ride to the dock, Chuck flagged the one taxi waiting at the end of the boardwalk. It was eight in the morning and no stores or restaurants were open yet. Two thousand frustrated travelers were about to inundate a slumbering Lahaina.

The driver dropped them off at the Napili Kai resort, where they rented snorkel gear. While Chuck prepared the masks, she peeled off her cover-up at water's edge and dove impulsively into the surf, feeling free and lithe as a dolphin. She surfaced and dove until Chuck gestured from the beach.

"You looked like a kid out there," he shouted.

"If only," she said as she clambered back ashore.

In the dining room that evening, the photographer approached. Chuck threw his arm around her and grinned as the man snapped their picture, but Nancy wasn't smiling. Instead, she was distracted by the fact that the sun had moved and was now setting on the wrong side of the ship.

"You're right," said Chuck. "That's odd."

"Would the lady like to order a beverage?" The waiter hovered, not mentioning their change in direction.

Just then, the PA crackled. They were informed that a passenger had given the "man overboard" alarm. Thus, the ship had turned around and was racing toward the sighting. The speaker assured everyone it was probably just an errant fishing buoy, and that they'd presently return to their original headings.

By the time they confirmed it was a false alarm and turned the ship back around, Nancy was on her third martini and did not care if they were sinking.

The next morning, she finished her shower and toweled off, ignoring the annoying but impotent shower drain which, eight days into their cruise, had done no more than gurgle. She pulled the door shut to deaden the sound and joined Chuck on the balcony for coffee. As soon as she became comfortably settled, they were interrupted by the PA, an unusual occurrence in one's stateroom and usually signifying an announcement of some import. Nancy listened closely, half-expecting to hear of mechanical difficulties.

The captain – the captain! Didn't he know how to delegate? – began speaking.

"Ladies and gentlemen, we hope you are having a wonderful morning aboard ship and enjoying our beautiful weather and calm seas. I apologize for this interruption, but we must ask for your help."

Was he going to ask them to row? Nancy stopped breathing.

"Unfortunately, one of your fellow passengers has fallen critically ill and is in need of blood." The captain explained that the man needed either O negative or A, and if any passenger possessing that blood type felt so inclined, might he or she present themselves at the infirmary for screening? The captain apologized again, wished them a happy voyage and signed off.

Nancy stared out across the ocean, her coffee forgotten. There she and Chuck sat on their balcony, enjoying the fresh air and calm seas, while a patient lay in the infirmary fighting for life. She had been so impatient and ungrateful.

The rest of that day and the next, she found herself thinking about the patient. Had anyone shown up to give blood? Had it helped? She wished she could have donated, but was of the wrong type. As the hours passed, she wondered how he was doing, and if the situation felt as depressing to the other passengers as it did to her. Would they ever hear of his progress? It was draining not to know. We need resolution, she thought. If the captain can get on the PA and whip us up, the least he can do is calm us down. What an idiot. What a bummer of a trip.

Two nights later, Chuck and Nancy stopped to listen to the after-dinner music emanating from the Atrium. They gazed over the railing at the three young women in evening gowns, playing Lara's Theme from Dr. Zhivago, using two violins and an accordion.

Suddenly the Captain's voice came over the PA. The musicians stopped playing. Passengers stopped talking. The ship fell silent. Nancy's hair prickled on the back of her neck. What now?

The young captain began by expressing felicitations and apologies for the interruption. He wanted to update everyone on the status of the passenger for whom he had requested blood. He was "still with us," the captain said, following a "massive response" from donors. The patient was recovering and had asked the captain to convey his gratitude.

"Thank God," Nancy said, reaching for Chuck's hand. "I'm glad he –"

"To be honest," the captain continued in a clipped British accent, "so many of you offered to donate that the infirmary had to turn people away. They were overwhelmed by your kindness, as am I. There is so much negativity in the world, and every day, one hears so much bad – but, well, this proves there is good, too. There is much to be grateful for. So on behalf of our passenger and his wife and children, and indeed the entire crew, we wish to express our appreciation to you, our guests. Again, please pardon the interruption, and enjoy the rest of your beautiful cruise."

Applause rose from the center of the ship, filling the atrium. Store clerks stepped out of their shops to join in. The music resumed; a sprightly number this time.

Nancy swiped at her eyes. "For God's sake," she said, fumbling for a tissue.

Just then the lights flickered and went off. Several passengers gasped, and one woman screamed. The lights blazed back on.

"Christ," Chuck said. "What a tub."

"She's an old ship," said Nancy. "I'm sure the captain's doing the best he can."

~ 8 ~

PHOENIX

"What do we have for lunch?" Gary hollered over the roar of Saturday morning football.

Stacey stopped brushing her hair and put her glasses back on. As loud as the TV was, she worried that the neighbors would be annoyed. She'd been raised in a silent house, where a television was considered wasteful frivolity.

Pulling her robe tighter, she went into the living room to answer his question.

"I made you a sandwich."

"What? Speak up." His eyes were trained on the television.

"There's a baloney sandwich in the fridge," she said. Since he got laid off, they were lucky to afford bread and lunchmeat at all. Lately most of their grocery budget went for beer.

"When are you gonna be home?"

"I shouldn't be more than a few hours."

"Why do you always have to work? You're not getting paid."

Stacey stood at the edge of the living room, staring at the hole in the heel of his left sock. "It's for a charity Evelyn supports, and when your boss asks you to help, you don't say no."

"I would have."

And that's why you can't keep a job, thought Stacey. They'd married young, before she'd realized she put more effort into selecting groceries than a husband. Now it was too late. She wasn't about to start over at fifty-three. "I won't be working alone. Two other ladies will be helping." When she pecked him on the cheek, she could smell nicotine on his skin, another no-no per his doctor whom they could no longer afford. "I'll be home in plenty of time to make dinner."

"Don't worry about it. I'll microwave something." Gary aimed the remote control at the TV.

At the bottom of the apartment stairs, trash whirled around her feet on a hot wind coming off the desert. In the car, the gas gauge blinked empty again. The last hundred times it happened, Gary said he forgot. Now she'd be late. Stacey backed out of the carport and headed for the Gas 'n Gulp.

Walking into the mini-mart, a man let the door close in her face. She got at the end of a long line, but when her turn came, the cashier slid the closed sign across the counter. Stacey moved over to the end of the second line, hoping Margaret and Ruth wouldn't get mad. Margaret had decided they would stuff the fundraising envelopes at her house in Palm Springs this weekend. That way they wouldn't have Evelyn breathing down their necks. Maybe they'd even drink wine, Margaret said, unaware that Stacey didn't drink anymore, having watched Gary deteriorate over the last twenty years.

Her stomach burned. The older she got, the worse her acid reflux bothered her. She dug in her purse for antacids. The idea of spending Saturday with Margaret and Ruth scared her. Mouthy old broads, they'd frequently go at each other at the store, or gang up on other workers. If she could have thought of an excuse fast enough, she'd have told Evelyn no.

But then that probably wouldn't have happened, either, because Stacey still wasn't comfortable using the word.

Forty minutes later, she found Margaret's gated community just off Highway 111. The gates stood open, unattended. Desert View sat baking in the April sunshine, a mobile home neighborhood with gravel front yards and palm trees. Metal sculptures of lizards and Kokopelli decorated every other house.

Stacey drove around on the circuitous streets, lost. Her outdated phone had no GPS, not like she'd have known how to use it anyway. One of these days she hoped to get a new smart phone, but at the moment she felt lucky to have a job, even if all she did was re-hang second-hand clothing from morning to night.

By some miracle she found Margaret's place. The triple-wide sat on a big lot on the edge of the golf course. The home looked even bigger than the house Stacey and Gary lived in before he got pink-slipped and they had to claim bankruptcy. By some rare good luck, Stacey had been able to find their affordable apartment in Banning.

She grabbed the supplies and slammed the trunk of her ancient Corolla, hoping the envelope-stuffing wouldn't take all day.

The address on the cement saguaro confirmed she was in the right place, but Stacey stood on the front porch knocking for a good five minutes without any response. Now her knuckles were copper-tinged, and every time she knocked on the rusty security screen, she had to angle her body to avoid the Palo Verde tree. Its lacey branches buzzed with bees, to which Stacey was allergic.

Nobody answered. Was it possible Margaret had forgotten? Or Stacey had the wrong day? Her calendar was buried in her purse. She set the box down.

"You can knock all you want but nobody's going to answer." Margaret, thirty feet away, took one last drag of her cigarette and ground the butt under her sandal. Her feet were bruised purple, and her toenails a bright red. "I haven't used that door in twenty years." She disappeared around the corner of the coach.

Stacey picked up the box and followed, ducking under thorny bougainvillea that draped over the carport. Inside the door of the house, her feet sank into super plush emerald green carpet. The house smelled of gardenia air freshener and fried bacon.

"Look who's here." Ruth was at the kitchen table, flipping through a box of envelopes, long acrylic nails flashing in the overhead light. "What took you?"

"I'm sorry," said Stacey. "I had to get gas, and couldn't find the house."

"We said eleven. Didn't we say eleven?"

"We've been waiting a half hour," said Margaret from the kitchen.

"I'm sorry," Stacey said again. "What can I do?"

"Did you bring the labels and the stamps?"

"I did." Stacey set the box down on the table.

"You want some tea, soft drink, water?" Margaret stood at the refrigerator, a pitcher of iced tea weighing down her scrawny brown arm. "Make up your mind. I don't have all day."

"Tea's fine, thanks."

"Thought you'd never decide."

"Get off her ass," said Ruth. "She came all the way out here."

"I'm fine," said Stacey, but they didn't seem to notice.

Margaret refilled Ruth's glass. "What'd I say? Did I say something wrong?"

"She doesn't have to be here," said Ruth.

"I know that."

"I'm sure she has things to do. Don't you, Stacey? I hope you have something better to do than sit around stuffing cancer envelopes with a couple old ladies." Ruth chuckled, her giant bosoms jiggling.

"Who you calling old?" said Margaret.

"Us. We're old."

Margaret glared at Stacey. "Do you think we're old?"

"Not at all."

Ruth pointed at a box. "Grab a bunch of envelopes and stick the labels where the return address goes. Then you can address them by hand."

"By hand?" asked Stacey.

"Are you deaf?" Ruth handed her a stack of envelopes. "They're already stuffed. We worked on them last night. Could've used your help then."

Head down, Stacey began peeling, sticking and writing.

"What's wrong with you?" Margaret sat down across from Ruth. "She's never going to come back, you keep talking like that."

"Like what?"

"Like you got a stick up your ass."

"You're the one with a stick up your ass."

Stacey looked at them, her mouth agape, but Ruth and Margaret sat grinning at each other.

"Don't mind her," said Margaret.

"Me?" Ruth finished a stack of envelopes. "You're the one with the problem."

"Is this a bad time?" Stacey asked.

"For what?" said Margaret. "We're just talking."

"Don't be so sensitive," said Ruth. "Ready for more?" She dumped a box of envelopes in front of Stacey.

"Holy shit. How many are there?" said Margaret. "We'll be here all day."

"At least it's for a good cause," said Stacey.

"Yeah, well, you ask me, Evelyn could've spent some of those donations on paid help instead of relying on us. Look at this." Margaret fanned a handful of envelopes in Stacey's direction. "It's like we're sending one to everybody on the planet. I should have told her where to get off."

"That'd go over well," said Ruth.

"Evelyn is pretty forceful," said Stacey.

"Forceful, my ass. She's a bitch." Ruth handed them each another stack of blanks. "But I need my job, just like you. So here we sit."

"I don't need this job. I'm independently wealthy." Margaret glared at Ruth.

"My ass."

"Yeah, your ass."

"Don't tell me my ass."

"Well, it's your ass, isn't it? It isn't my ass."

Stacey had stopped working.

"Something wrong with you?" said Margaret.

"Nothing wrong with her. Leave her alone." Ruth looked at Stacey. "Is there something wrong with you?"

"I don't understand you guys," said Stacey.

"What? What's to understand?"

"I mean, you act like you're unhappy."

"Who's unhappy?" Margaret said.

"We're not unhappy. This is us, happy," said Ruth.

"Yeah, you should see us unhappy. If we were unhappy, you'd know it."

Stacey ducked her head. "I'm just saying."

"What are you saying?"

"You make me uncomfortable with all your bickering."

"So, big deal. We bicker," said Ruth.

"But only when we're happy. You should see us mad." Margaret got up from the table. "Who's hungry? I got ham sandwiches and chips. And if you can keep from being a pain in the ass, I got cookies for dessert."

"Just bring the cookies and shut up." Ruth grinned at Stacey. "See? It's how we talk."

"It's weird."

"So what? We're weird."

They stopped for lunch. Outside, Margaret spread a plastic tablecloth on the patio table and handed out napkins and sandwiches. A warm desert breeze rustled the palm trees shading the patio. On the fairway, a foursome rolled past in golf carts, one sporting a blue handicapped flag.

Margaret watched them go by. "If he's so handicapped, why's he playing golf?"

"What do you care?" said Ruth.

"I know the sumbitch, and he's no more handicapped than I am."

Stacey took a bite of her sandwich. Then a bee started going after her lunch. She waved it away. It came back. She waved her napkin at it, more forcefully, and the bee took off. "Good sandwich. Thanks," she said to Margaret.

"It's no big deal, just meat and lettuce."

"Still, thanks."

Margaret shrugged. "Eat more. You're too skinny."

Stacey smiled. "Thank you." The bee came back. She waved it away. It persisted.

"It's not a compliment," said Margaret. "You look like you never eat. Don't you ever eat?"

"I'm eating now."

"Yeah, well, have some more chips." Margaret shoved the bag closer to Stacey.

"I'm fine." Stacey put down her sandwich and flailed with both hands at the bee.

"You're fine? What's that mean? Eat."

"It means she doesn't want to eat. If she doesn't want to eat, she doesn't have to eat," said Ruth, biting into her sandwich. "Get off her ass."

"I'm not on her ass. I just think she should eat," said Margaret.

"I don't want to fucking eat!" Stacey smashed the bee with her shoe.

Ruth stopped chewing.

Margaret grinned. "Fine. So then don't eat."

"I won't."

Margaret stood up. "Who wants wine?"

"I do," said Stacey. "And pass me the chips."

~ 9 ~

BAD ADVICE

Carolyn jumped when the heavy folder landed on her desk. "You're going to interview Amanda Westfield," said Rich, her editor. "She'll meet you tomorrow morning." He bent down and spoke quietly into her ear. "I'm feeling the need for a staff meeting."

Wincing, Carolyn leaned away. "Did you go to the taco place for lunch?"

Rich walked back to his office, laughing. With his angular frame and thick silver hair, he gave off a sense of vitality she envied. Even though twenty years older than Carolyn, at sixty he was sure of the universe and his place in it.

At Starbucks the next morning, she studied the other customers. Men stood in line, jingling the contents of their pockets and speaking loudly to their earbuds. Women jittered from foot to foot, balancing on six-inch heels while clutching laptops and digging through shoulder bags. Carolyn took a tiny sip of plain coffee. She never ordered the fancy varieties because she thought doing so was unethical while people were out there in the world starving. For this reason, and also the fact that she couldn't afford it, she never came here except in the rare event she had to meet someone for her work. Thus she felt uncomfortable with the clever conventions and verbal shorthand with which one ordered.

The fan over the door roared, announcing the arrival of Amanda Westfield. Carolyn barely recognized the overweight woman from her photos on the Internet. She wore a black designer pantsuit and an Hermès scarf. Diamond rings on both hands cut into fat fingers.

Carolyn stood and the women shook hands. Amanda set her large Fendi bag on the coffee table and dropped into the matching chair. Air escaped from the cushions with a loud whoosh. "I don't have much time. Would you order for me? Venti double dirty chai latte with whipped cream. And a chocolate chip cookie. Two."

Standing in line, Carolyn felt self-conscious in her drooping, oversized tunic and scuffed flats. In the Valley at this time of year, most of the rich people escaped the growing heat for second homes in cooler climes, leaving the working stiffs behind. As a result, the dress code began to relax and would stay that way until October, when the Season resumed.

When Carolyn set the chai down, Amanda said, "You're not the same person I spoke with before."

"No, that was Sandra. She resigned. I'm filling in, finishing up her assignments." Carolyn's shoulders rounded in their customary slump. "I'm actually the advice columnist for the Bee."

"Carolyn's Corner? That's you?"

"You've read it?"

"I wouldn't miss it," Amanda said. "It's compelling."

Carolyn sat up straighter. "So, about your season opener, when Sandra left off you were describing the gala to raise money for student scholarships. How many donors do you think will attend?"

Amanda shifted on her massive bottom, attempting to cross her legs. "Probably a couple thousand, give or take."

"Can you give me names?"

"The usual crowd. Go to your archives and regurgitate any of my past events. It's always the same people. Dr. So-and-So and his voluptuous new wife, Tiffany or Brittany or something. And the same old former world leaders, slobbering in their soup. So tedious."

Carolyn raised her eyebrows. "But you're putting poor students through college."

"Of course." Amanda waved a hand dismissively, her diamonds flashing. "I'm just saying, it's boring. But, you. I would think being an advice columnist would be extremely interesting. All that destructive behavior to fix."

"So anyway," Carolyn said, clicking her pen, "how much money do you expect to raise this season?"

"Again, the usual. One thirty, one forty."

"Thousand?"

"At least." Amanda licked a bit of a whipped cream from the edge of the cup.

"Good Lord."

"Don't get excited. We practically have to beg the high schools to participate. With all the do-gooders in the valley, they're drowning in scholarships. The kids can't be bothered to apply. So there the money sits, drawing interest."

"That's appalling," said Carolyn.

"Yes, it is, but we can't admit it. If it weren't for poor people, there'd be no parties to go to and show off our clothes."

Carolyn studied her notepad.

"I'll have my assistant email all the docs for the article. Now let's talk about you. What's the most scandalous letter you've come across lately?"

"I don't really get scandalous. More like heartbreaking."

"Okay, the one that bothered you the most." Amanda settled in, waiting.

Carolyn stared across the shop at a young woman reading a book while her infant slept in its stroller. Why should she tell Amanda anything? She was a voyeur, wanting to escape her luxe life with a dive to the bottom to see what was down there. Yet there was something about her obesity that made her seem more down-to-earth. "There was this one – yesterday – about a single mother with six kids who doesn't have a car and has to use the laundromat." She dug in her briefcase. "I printed it out. Here." She smoothed it out on the table.

Amanda leaned forward to read the letter, and Carolyn noticed her perfume. She inhaled the golden, sparkling fragrance. Instantly, her mind filled with images of yellow and white-striped chaise lounges next to a deep blue infinity pool on a cliff overlooking the ocean; a tropical drink, a big floppy hat, and a deeply tanned pool boy attending to her every wish.

Amanda's voice startled Carolyn out of her travel-magazine reverie. "So she has to use the public laundry a couple days a week. Why is that an issue?"

"It is a pretty big deal. When you're poor, life is expensive. You might not pay in terms of money, but time is just as costly, sometimes even more so. I don't know if you read the whole thing, but she spends hours away from her children, doing laundry. She can't afford a babysitter, so the older ones get into mischief while she's gone. She already got evicted once because the kids flooded their apartment."

"Why doesn't she buy a cheap, used washer and hang the clothes outside to dry?"

Carolyn wondered if the woman was so accustomed to privilege she couldn't fathom the actual world of the less fortunate. "Like I said, it's an apartment."

"She could get a second job."

"Did you not see the last paragraph?" Carolyn turned the letter around and Amanda leaned closer, reading.

"Okay, I see your point. She's working two jobs and attending night school. That makes a difference. You have to give her credit." Amanda tapped one finger on her cheek. "Listen, I could help. I'll buy her a washer and dryer out of the scholarship fund."

Carolyn drew back. "Is that legal?"

"It's to help the mother go to school, right?"

"Are you serious? That would be great! What do we do, mail her a check?"

"Slow down." Amanda's eyes twinkled. "You have to do it a certain way or all the poor people in town will be chasing after me. I'll have my guy arrange to buy and deliver the set anonymously. You've got my email. Send me her address." She glanced at her watch. "I have to go. This was fun. Let's visit again, sometime soon. You can bring more letters."

Carolyn watched her leave. Ordinarily, she didn't trust the very rich, but Amanda had demonstrated a soft side. Maybe she simply hadn't been exposed to true poverty, but was open to learning and growth in that regard. It would be nice to think so. Lately the world had seemed so very harsh and brutal, and Carolyn was hungry for any sign of hope, no matter how miniscule. She gathered up her notebook and pencils and walked out to the parking lot.

That afternoon, she sat at her computer to finish the article. She revised and revised, working until hunger prevented her from making any more changes. She opened her email program to send it to Rich.

He had sent her a message. Staff meeting tomorrow night, 8 pm, at Westlake. It was Rich's little joke. Westlake was the complex where he kept an apartment while his divorce played out, and out, and out. He and Carolyn had been sneaking around for almost five years. Although Carolyn sometimes felt taken advantage of, at her age and in the desert environment of plastic this and fake that, she wasn't interested in competing. Rich might not be available, but he was funny and energetic. She sent an email telling him yes.

Amanda's assistant had also sent an email, saying Amanda

had time next Thursday morning, if Carolyn wanted to meet. She replied quickly in the affirmative, wondering about Amanda's perfume and if they had free samples at Saks.

While she ate a bowl of leftover soup, Carolyn found herself seeing the kitchen through Amanda's eyes. Admittedly, the place could benefit from a good straightening. After finishing the bottle of chardonnay, Carolyn emptied and reloaded the dishwasher. While that ran, she swept and mopped the floor and emptied the trash. Finally, counters and sink sparkling, she ran a mop around all flat surfaces, dusting and shining. That night, she fell into bed, uncharacteristically pleased with herself.

Over the next few days, she sorted through the incoming letters, watching for those that Amanda might find interesting. At times, however, a letter would surface that would remind her that this job wasn't about fun. It was about helping troubled people, and the same doubts would surface. For example, last December, a young man had written, despondent over the fact that he could only escape suicidal depression when lighting fires. Had Carolyn's words helped him? How could they? Because who was she to be handing out advice? Although she'd survived her share of hard knocks, and matured beyond foolishness, she was no therapist. The advice column had landed in her lap when the previous woman quit, another clerical worker whom management pushed into the job. The pay was low, so they couldn't expect to hire a licensed professional, but Carolyn wanted to help, and she needed the money, insignificant as it was. Rich had asked her to take the job as a personal favor to him.

At first she felt inadequate but as months passed, she began to receive follow-up letters from those she'd helped. The writer might say Carolyn was a life-saver, or that her advice was brilliant. Her confidence grew, and her fear of harming someone faded. She began to feel, for the first time in her life, that her work mattered.

At their next meeting, Amanda arrived carrying a computer

tablet. "Wait until you see this," she said, tapping the screen. "My guy filmed it. Look! Mamacita's crying, and all the kids are hugging her."

"This feels really good," said Carolyn. "Thank you so much."

"I even signed the washer."

"It was supposed to be anonymous."

Amanda laughed. "Don't worry. I put our initials in black sharpie, on the back, where they'll never see it, and even if they did, they won't make the connection. A & C. That could be anyone. What else do you have?"

Carolyn blushed. "Really?"

"Of course. The foundation has a ton of money, and better it go for people who appreciate a hand up than those ungrateful students."

"Well, I do have one." Carolyn pulled a letter out of her purse. "There's this man who just got out of prison."

"Prison!"

"But he was falsely convicted. That group, the Innocence Project? They got him out, but now he has to start his life all over again, and he's already in his middle forties."

"I've heard of this happening, but I thought it was a scam," Amanda said.

"It really happens. Here's proof." Carolyn unfolded the letter and pressed it flat.

After reading it, Amanda looked up. "It sounds credible. Consider me a believer." She would buy the man a new wardrobe and a seasonal bus pass from the scholarship fund.

"Thank you," Carolyn said.

At their next meeting, Amanda had Carolyn order a skim latte for her, and no cookie. After looking through several letters, Amanda chose two, and later she arranged for a child's dental work, and a year's rent for two impoverished retirees.

The week after, she paid for two sisters to attend community college.

A week later, she found money for a terminally ill father to take his family to a resort.

The next week, she bought a used car for a hardworking mother.

Carolyn exclaimed more than once at Amanda's generosity, but her friend shrugged it off. "It's exciting to help," she said. "We're improving humanity, one family at a time."

That night, Carolyn met Rich at Westlake, and they had sex, unsatisfying for her, but tonight she didn't care. Afterward, she told Rich about her secret project.

"I'd be leery," he said. "People like her take advantage. She'll use you."

"We're doing charitable works for the community. I'm only acting as her scout. How can that be bad?"

"Think about it." He fell asleep as he said it.

Carolyn let herself out.

Eight weeks into their project, Amanda said, "I'm having a birthday party on St. Barts at the end of the month. Want to come?"

"I'm not sure-"

"It's my treat. Besides, you'll be working. I intend to brainstorm with you and my team over an idea, a new organization dedicated to helping those in need, based on your letters. You'll be on my board, with a big fat salary. If you're interested, that is." Amanda stood. In contrast to her first appearance, she radiated energy. Her black pantsuits had vanished in favor of sleek linen slacks and colorful blouses, and her skin had cleared up. "See you next Thursday?"

Carolyn nodded, speechless. Ten minutes after the chauffeur closed the car door and drove Amanda away, Carolyn remained in her seat, considering the possibilities.

* * * * *

Back at her office in the Thornton Building, Amanda felt energized. This was the change she needed. Every morning now, she popped out of bed, hungry for breakfast prepared by her live-in chef, and ready for an exhaustive workout with Sven, her trainer. She liked the way she felt and the way she looked. In another week or two, her personal shopper would deliver an entirely new wardrobe, each item tailored for her slimmed-down frame. This season, she would flatten the competition. The Valley would know who was in charge, who was top dog on the philanthropic pyramid.

"Stocks up?" Brent, her friend and fellow member of the board, stood in her doorway, his blond hair falling into his eyes. "You're grinning like a starlet at the Academy Awards."

"Come in. I have something fabulous to tell you. Close the door." After two months of secret philanthropy, she couldn't keep it to herself anymore, but Brent was discreet.

He sprawled in a wingchair, his loafers propped on an ottoman. "Spill it, girlfriend." After listening to her breathless description, he chuckled. "It's a sucker bet."

"You're wrong. These aren't a bunch of spoiled kids. They're hard-working adults who don't have a prayer of their situation improving. I can make a little tweak and change their lives forever."

"I doubt it."

"How can you be so cynical?"

"Just realistic, luv."

"You're a wet blanket." Amanda pouted. This wasn't the reaction she'd hoped for. She wished she hadn't opened her mouth.

"Don't be glum, chum. Maybe you're right." Brent leaned forward, suddenly interested. "Hey, I have an idea. How about a little wager - your optimism against my pessimism? Let's see if your money changes anything with those people."

"How would we know that?"

"Hmm." Brent snapped his fingers. "Say, remember when Walker was diddling around in the cash drawer, and we had him investigated?"

Amanda nodded. It wasn't strictly legal, of course, but the results had been an eye opener. Walker was swiftly dealt with by some of Austin's less-than-savory associates. "We could use that P.I."

"Yes. I'll set it up. We'll have him do a little sleuthing. Say, two weeks. If the majority of your families have been improved by your generosity, I'll owe you. If not, you pay up. Fifty grand to the winner?"

They shook, and Brent left to make the arrangements.

* * * * *

Carolyn couldn't understand why Amanda had begged off their usual Thursday meetings at Starbucks. For the past two weeks, her assistant had made one thin excuse after another.

Finally, Amanda agreed to meet. She declined Carolyn's offer of coffee.

"You know those people we've been helping? I had someone follow up on them," said Amanda. "Seventeen of the twenty items we donated were either pawned or sold outright, and when we gave them cash grants, they used them for alcohol, drugs, and fantasy football. Of the three cars we donated, one person got a job but she had an attitude problem and got fired. One drove drunk and totaled the car, and now he's disabled. The third one used hers to start a housecleaning business, but her kids ran wild while she was at work so she quit, and her new ex-boyfriend stole the car." Amanda folded the paper from which she'd been reading.

Carolyn's face burned. "It's discouraging. I expected better."

"I think we should table our project."

"Our new foundation?"

"Yes, and anything else we talked about." Amanda stood and gathered her purse and notebook. "Goodbye."

Carolyn couldn't move. The air grow heavier. The people in

Starbucks looked toward the vanishing Amanda, and then back at Carolyn as if expecting her to stand and deliver an explanation. She walked over to the windows and watched the limousine glide into traffic and disappear.

Carolyn called her office, reported that she was sick, and went home. Feeling lethargic, she lay on the bed hoping to nap, but sleep evaded her and she finally rose, rumpled and exhausted. In the afternoon she fixed a cup of vegetable soup, but had no appetite and poured it down the sink. She stared out her window, past the carport and the row of dumpsters to where a flock of pigeons roosted and pooped, shaded from the glaring desert sun.

Rich sent her an email. Staff meeting tonight? She deleted it.

Back at the office the next day, she opened her email and reviewed the new batch of letters. Every writer's plea for advice sounded like it was written by a con or a hopeless loser. Carolyn trolled the newspaper website, hoping to find a feel-good story, something to motivate her, some source of inspiration. While perusing the society section, she saw Amanda had started a foundation to rescue greyhounds. Amanda wore a black pantsuit. It looked tight.

Carolyn watched the newsroom clock, its hands creeping interminably toward noon. Finally she couldn't take it anymore. She carried the last of her work to Rich's office.

He sat behind his desk, scowling. "Didn't you get my email yesterday? I waited but you never showed."

She flopped down in a chair. "I didn't feel well."

"You're moping about that Amanda woman."

"I'm fine."

"You look like hell. I would say I'm sorry, but I warned you," said Rich. "Get a grip. Your work is suffering."

So am I, thought Carolyn. For one brief summer, she'd begun to believe in people again.

"Hey, you know what I'm thinking?" Rich gave her a

crooked smile. "I'm thinking you need a good cheering up tonight."

Without answering, she returned to her cubicle to box up her things. On her monitor, breaking news shouted at her.

Somewhere in the world, a madman had kidnapped two hundred schoolgirls from a Nigerian high school to use as sex slaves for his rebel army.

Somewhere in the United States, two billionaire industrialist brothers, declaring that climate change was in fact real and irreversible, announced they were resigned to the truth and would thus accelerate their construction of coal-fired power plants.

And somewhere in America, a domestic car company, having determined that the loss of human life was cheaper than an equipment recall, declined to warn its customers about fatal risk associated with its product, with predictable results.

She reached around the back of the monitor and hit the off switch.

When Carolyn stepped outside, the desert sun warmed her skin and bees buzzed in the Palo Verde trees shading the parking lot. Two young women in bright summer dresses sashayed past, laughing under big colorful hats. As they walked in front of Carolyn's car, they waved, and almost against her will, Carolyn's hand slowly lifted and she waved back, responding in a language the three of them shared. The women continued walking, the Palo Verdes continued swaying, the bees pollinated, cars whizzed past on the street in front of her. There was nothing she could do, and yet, she could do this: she could keep putting one foot in front of the other, she could wave, smile, and breathe. She could find a new job and companionship. She could make a difference, even if that difference were limited to the confines of her small but precious life.

On the way home, she stopped at the Goodwill to look for something cheery to brighten her wardrobe. Something that another woman, one with a fatter wallet, may have dropped off.

As Carolyn passed a row of second-hand appliances, she heard a giggle. A wispy blond girl in shorts and a tee shirt pointed at the back of a used washing machine. "Look, somebody put a heart here. A & C. How cute."

Carolyn slunk closer, feigning interest in a dryer. A sales clerk approached the girl. "Can I help you?"

"I'd like to buy this. I mean, he would. For me." The girl looked up from under her lashes and blushed at the old man who stood near her, thumbs hooked into his overalls.

"I'm from her church," said the man. "We use member donations to help those who are less fortunate."

"This is my first washing machine," said the girl, pulling on twin braids. "Can you tell me how to use it?"

The clerk shook his head. "Sorry, we just sell them."

The old man spotted Carolyn lurking nearby. "Excuse me, ma'am, I wonder if you might be able to explain this device to her?"

Carolyn spun around, caught. "You just –" she began, then stopped. She looked from the clerk, to the old man, to the girl, and shrugged.

"No, I'm sorry," she said. "I can't help you."

~ 10 ~

AN INNOCENT MAN

I was a poor girl, and I married a rich man. My heart almost stopped when I found out how easy things were going to be. But rich or poor, I'm still me, so right after our wedding, I analyzed our budget. See, before we met, I watched every penny. You had to, in my line of work, because the pay varied so much from week to week. In my twenties and thirties, I was a masseuse. A lot of the time we'd be sitting around doing nothing, so when the other girls had a chance to do extra and make big bucks, they would. Which was fine for them, but I'm not that way. Eventually I saved enough to go to a school where they taught you office skills, and I landed a job at the DMV. I never made much, but in a lot of ways it was better.

So I got in the habit of tracking my money – okay, budgeting, which sounds fussy, but there wasn't anything fussy about my system, just a plain old hand-drawn chart on a piece of cardboard. That's how I knew what was coming in and going out every month. It covered a whole year at a glance. If you have one of those, you can plan ahead for the big expenses, like car insurance or whatever, and with the way I used to live, "whatever" meant taking care of every stray dog and human that wandered through. So I always tracked everything, and that's why, when Hank and I fell in love, I didn't owe anything and my life was in good shape.

When we got married, right away I wanted to get a handle on my new situation. Hank said not to worry about it, but I couldn't help it. "How much do we make?" I asked him. It was hard to ask because he was a rich person, and I came from the other side of the tracks, so it felt kind of rude, but I kept at him, and after a while I realized he didn't know.

"How can you not know?"

"It varies," he said. Depending on how much they made in annual profits, the partner compensation was applied to that. The big brother of the family did all the accounting and didn't share his calculations with anybody.

"What happens if your income goes way down?" I asked.

"It does. It goes up and down from year to year, but we've always been fine." He was floating on a raft in our pool, drifting toward the little waterfall coming out of the hot tub. For a man just turned fifty, he was in great shape, still tall and tanned. "We'll always be okay," he said.

"But what if they cut off your cars or medical or...?"

He laughed at me, his sunglasses glinting. "Don't worry about it, babe. If anything that bad ever happened, it'd mean the whole country was in trouble."

Of course, that's exactly what happened, and pretty soon there wasn't enough to go around. The brother's kids were sporting new boats and Escalades while the rest of the family, including Hank and me, were told not to expect much. So we got out. We sold our house in Newport Beach and moved to Pleasantville, a blue-collar town an hour east. Pleasantville reminded me of my roots, so I was happy as hell. No longer did I feel like I had to get a facelift before going to the grocery store, but I did worry about what it was going to do to Hank. The man has pink hands. He's never worked a day in his life, doing physical labor I mean.

But he surprised me. He settled right in, trying out the local greasy spoons and crowing about how much we were saving on property taxes. Cracked me up. One of his strong points is he's flexible, but sometimes I wonder what goes on in his head. He grew up sheltered by wealth, and the stuff he says sometimes makes no sense at all. Like he used to say if he started to lose his mind or his bodily functions when he got old that he was going to "go into L.A., score some drugs, and O.D." I let him talk the first few times he said it, but one day I got mad and told him he was being stupid, and he'd more likely get robbed and killed before he got ten feet in. I told him to forget it, that I'd take care of him, no matter how bad he got. He put his fingers on my scar just then, when I said that. He did that sometimes, when he was sad for how I used to live.

But that was no big deal to me. Some jerk cut me, trying to steal my week's earnings from the massage parlor, but I shot him and he ran off. Now Hank, he doesn't know the first thing about protecting himself.

Like the time we stayed at a motel in Fontana. I know what you're thinking. Why would anybody stay in Fontana? But I have family there. One day my sister threw a party that ran late, and we didn't feel like sleeping on the floor of her house with the other relatives, so we went to a motel.

When we checked in, I got a bad feeling. It was one of two rooms on the back end of the place, behind the rest of the complex. They were the only rooms where the doors opened directly onto the back parking lot instead of the courtyard. I could see right away it was a drug dealer's delight.

"We were lucky to get this," Hank said. "It's a big race weekend. Every motel in town is sold out."

I kept my mouth shut. No sense worrying him, too. There was a hard thump against the wall and then some drunken hyena started laughing.

"Can you sleep with the AC on?" I asked. The air in the room was stuffy, but I mainly wanted to drown out the noise.

"No problem." He got in bed.

I waited until Hank started snoring two seconds after he lay down, and then I dragged the desk over to where it blocked the door. See, I knew this place, or places like it. In my youth I flirted with drugs and such, and my husbands were drug-addled themselves, and one beat me for fun, until I grew a pair and left. So as soon as I saw what we were dealing with here at the motel, my guard was up because I knew what could happen if things went bad.

All night long, I kept waking up and peeking through the drapes and the peephole in the door, watching cars pull in and out of our parking lot. The door to the next room opened and slammed every ten or fifteen minutes. I heard a baby crying and sharp voices from time to time. I hoped nobody got mad enough to start shooting through the thin walls. I also hoped, if there was a raid, that Hank and I looked middle-aged and innocent enough that the cops would give us a pass. I fell asleep and had a nightmare that I had to divorce Hank because he was a drug dealer. In the morning, I woke up crying.

Hank heard me rustling around and rolled over, eyes bright. "I slept great. Are you hungry?"

I sat up, shaky from bad sleep and bad memories. "Sure."

"How about we try that Denny's down the street? Is Denny's good?"

As we left the hotel, I couldn't look at the other room. It was quiet, but all I could think about was how that baby had cried all night.

At the restaurant, Hank politely asked the waitress to describe a Grand Slam breakfast. "Is that popular?" he asked. I could tell she wanted to laugh in his face, but when she saw the look on mine, she behaved herself.

Before I met Hank, life was hard, and I learned to take care of those who look out for me. Also, he taught me things, like how to use a napkin properly, and to say pardon me when I shoved past somebody.

When Hank first came up to my window at the DMV, I was surprised at how nice he was, and he made me laugh. The next day he came back, and the day after that, each time pretending he had a new problem with his registration. It seemed funny to me that this guy, he was in his late forties by that point, seemed like he was flirting with me. Because I'm six years older and no beauty. But I'm in good shape and I look okay with the right makeup and a nice outfit.

He talked me into having lunch with him. I picked a workday so I'd have an excuse to bolt if need be, but it went well. We did that a few times, then kicked it up to dinner and a movie. He was always a gentleman except when he'd let this kind of sarcastic, funny, dark side slip out, and oh my God, he made me laugh so hard. When that happened, I started liking him more and more, and we went on a lot of dates. He even taught me how to drive his boat. And then, before I could say holy shit are you kidding me? we were engaged. Got married at a little place out in the country. His family didn't show up but mine did, and they ate and drank enough for both families.

But anyway, right then I looked at that waitress's face, one side of her smile turned down like she was laughing inside. She had no way of knowing what a fine person she was looking at.

Hank dug into his pancakes like he does everything, with appreciation. He ate every bit.

"That was delicious," he said, holding the door open for me on the way out. The air felt cool, a bit of dampness left over from the night making everything fresh. "I would have that again."

From what I've told you, you'd think he's lived a charmed life but he's had hardships just like the rest of us. Only thing is, good, bad, up, down, he just sees it as life, whereas I'm the worrier. But maybe I take it too far.

And how much time do you have anyway? Isn't it like wasting something good, to be always on guard against the bad?

What if it never happens? You do all that worrying for nothing.

He opened my car door, but before I got in, I put my hands on his chest. "You know what I'm thinking?" I said. "We should get out more, treat ourselves a little better. Spend some money. Maybe go on up the coast. Take Highway 1. Do a road trip."

He didn't argue, of course. Gave me a big, warm smile, so I moved in close for a hug.

~ 11 ~

BOARDING HOUSE

D oris pulled the curtain aside and squinted at the late-afternoon light. Yes, a man was definitely outside hammering, pounding a sign into her lawn. She drained the last glass of the last bottle of her ex's prized wine collection and opened the front door.

Hearing it squeak, the man stopped. A hammer dangled from his blue-veined hand.

"What is this?" She tore the paper off the stick and tried to read it without her glasses.

"A legal notice." The man glared at her, his bushy eyebrows twitching. "The HOA Board hereby informs you that you're in violation of code." Doris' driveway was littered with folding tables that were mounded with clothing and stacked with dusty books and magazines. Cardboard boxes sagged in the late afternoon light. Ragged towels and tablecloths spilled onto the cement.

The man pointed at a campaign sign advertising Doris' liberal candidate. "In addition, your signage does not comply with Board rules."

"Who the hell are you, little man?"

"Austin Stonebreaker, Board Member. He stood up straighter. "I recently moved in down the street, and I object to the derelict appearance of your property."

The idea that an HOA presided over the place made Doris laugh. Her neighborhood, a cluster of oversized two-stories in the foothills northwest of Cathedral City, had been deteriorating for years.

Angie, a blind golden retriever, wandered over from next door. She sat down next to Doris, leaned against her leg, and woofed in the general direction of Austin Stonebreaker.

"You can also be cited for violating the leash laws in this community."

Doris rubbed the dog's ears. "She's not mine."

"Nevertheless." Stonebreaker pointed at the sign. "I have done my duty and you have been warned. You have ten days to remove your garbage. After that, the Board will remove it for you and send you the bill."

"That's nice. Now get off my lawn."

"But you're in violation -"

"I don't give a shit. Get off my property." Doris shooed Angie home and then, robe flapping, turned her back on the man and went inside, where she watched him from the peephole. Stonebreaker retrieved the legal notice, reattached it to the stick and gave that a final smack with the hammer. Scowling, he pulled the campaign sign out of the ground, tore it in half, and marched into the street just as the Big Black Truck turned the corner and roared past. Stonebreaker flailed backwards in terror and fell to the pavement.

Doris gasped and ran back outside, her fluffy slippers catching in the ankle-high grass. She grasped the neighbor's elbow and helped him to his feet.

"Goddamn! Goddamn!" His elbow was bleeding through his shirt.

"You're lucky. One day he's going to kill somebody."

"He almost did. The community should take action. Do you know who he is?"

Doris didn't. The windows were tinted so she couldn't see the driver, but assumed it was a man, probably young. She'd seen him run stop signs, tailgate other vehicles, and harass fellow drivers. Stonebreaker was right – the situation was intolerable. What if he slammed into another vehicle, maybe even an SUV with a young family inside? No amount of after-the-fact justice would bring them back. She wished she were a policeman, and could arrest him, throw him to the pavement, and maybe kick him around a bit.

"Can you walk?" she asked.

"I'm fine." The neighbor shook off Doris' grip. "You should read that notice. Every day matters. If you wait too long, it could get very expensive."

Back inside, Doris opened another bottle of wine and a bag of tortilla chips. In the living room, she turned on the black and white TV, bought for ten dollars at the Goodwill after selling Harry's flat-screen for two hundred. She surfed around until she found a rerun of I Love Lucy.

Doris put her feet up on the coffee table and noticed the bits of grass and leaves clinging to her slippers. She kicked them off, thinking she should probably shower sometime today, but what the hell. Nobody around to notice. Maybe tomorrow. She crammed a chip in her mouth and watched Ethyl trying to distract Ricky while Lucy attempted to fish the wallet out of his pocket.

When she heard a series of knocks on the door, Doris aimed the remote at the TV and turned up the volume. The pounding continued. "Mom, are you in there? Open up!"

Doris hid the wine glass beside the sofa and went to the front door. Her son Jack stood on the porch. "Hi, honey."

"How come you don't answer the phone? I've been calling for days."

"Nice to see you too. Did you have dinner yet?" Doris closed the door and headed toward the kitchen.

Jack followed her. "Did your housekeeper quit?"

"Can I offer you a Coors?"

He sat at the kitchen table. "What's with all the junk in the driveway? And there's dog poop in the yard."

"That's Angie. She forgets which house is hers."

"But the driveway?"

"I'm having a yard sale."

"The grass is a foot deep. You should get on Santos."

"Santos doesn't work for me anymore, and I don't have a lawn mower." She set an unopened beer in front of him and went back to the refrigerator.

Jack glanced at the pile of dirty dishes in the sink. "Maybe it's time to sell. Get something smaller and more manageable."

At the counter, Doris picked apart an old ham sandwich, extracting the meat and setting it on a napkin.

"I talked to Dad last night," said Jack. "It's hard for him too, you know, with both mortgages."

She picked up the napkin and opened the back door. At the far end of the wooden deck, she deposited the meat into a dog dish, wiped her fingers on the napkin and whistled. At the edge of the yard, where it sloped downward toward Palm Springs, a creosote bush rustled as a feral housecat appeared. The cat licked her chops and waited for Doris to go back inside, but Doris paused to savor the view. Her eyes swept the purple and golden reach of the valley, as the sun lowered and the heat of the late October afternoon began to dissipate. The distant hills turned from rose to chocolate, and shadows deepened in the crevasses of the Little San Bernardino Mountains to the east.

Jack tapped on the kitchen window, questioning Doris with his eyes. She went back inside, and together they stood by the sink, watching the cat devour the meat. "Do you ever think about selling?" he asked.

"Jack, please." She wiped the counter and shook out the

dish rag.

"Seriously, what do you need with six bedrooms? And all those bathrooms?"

"It's not a question of what I need. I like it here, and I'm not going to move just because your father left. Besides, I'm too old to change."

"You're not that old." He slung his arm around her as they faced the window. "Come on. You're doing great for your age, but I'm just worried about the years ahead. It's not going to get any easier." He trailed after Doris into the living room. "You could probably make enough to afford a little townhouse."

"No, I can't." She looked at him over her reading glasses, patched with electrical tape. "I'm under water, and I'm behind in my payments."

"But Dad–"

"He stopped paying two years ago. When I had my surgery."

"Jesus." He scrubbed at his face. "How are you getting by?"

"As you can see, I have yard sales. I also sub teach at the high school a couple days a week."

"Those kids are animals."

"The children are very nice." She had to send one of her mini-skirted students home yesterday. Evidently, the girl had forgotten her panties. And the day before that, Doris nearly had to break up a knife-fight.

"You can't be earning enough to make the payments."

"It's enough if I'm careful." She fixed him with one of her stares. "I enjoy the space, and the yard, and the view. It's quiet here. I can sleep at night. This house has a lot of memories for me. Doesn't it for you?"

"That's not the point." The sweep of his hand took in the denuded walls and empty rooms. "This is no way to live."

Doris sat quietly fuming. She'd been lonely but now she wished Jack would leave.

"Anyway, I came over to tell you we're going camping this weekend, up in Joshua Tree. Rebecca's worried about Brandon.

Says he spent the whole summer hiding in his room. She wants him to get outside and play like a normal kid."

"Teenagers don't play. They sulk."

Jack sighed. "So, about camping. Becks thought you might want to come along."

"I haven't camped in years."

"Why does that matter? We've got everything you need. Sleeping bag, tent, air mattress. It'll be good for you to get out." He hugged her, resting his chin on her head.

Doris closed her eyes, enjoying the embrace. It would be good to spend time with Brandon, and she needed to make more of an effort with Rebecca. "Just the weekend?"

"Two nights. That's it."

"All right."

* * * * *

The campfire popped and sizzled, and Doris looked up in time to see a shooting star arcing away into darkness. Next to her, Brandon hunched over his iPad, lank hair hanging in his face. Rebecca walked over and stood in front of him, hands planted on big sturdy hips. "Please turn that thing off."

"Why? I'm not doing anything wrong."

"Turn it off," she said. "You're out here in all this beauty."

"Nothing beautiful out here. Buncha dead trees and rocks."

Jack poked a stick at the fire. "You can live without it for a few hours."

Brandon muttered a curse, then looked up. "Sorry, Grandma."

"I didn't hear anything." Doris reached over and brushed the hair out of his eyes. "What's so interesting?"

He angled the tablet away from his parents. "They even have recipes," he said, showing her the bomb-making website.

Doris' eyebrows rose. "Ah."

"You're interested in cooking?" said Rebecca. "Let me see."

Brandon snapped the tablet closed. "You told me to turn it off."

"Let's get some rest." Jack stood and stretched. "I want to get an early start tomorrow."

"If you don't feel like going, you could hang around camp," Rebecca said to Doris. "The hike is pretty rugged."

Doris winced at the condescension in Rebecca's voice. "Piece of cake."

"I don't want to go on your crappy hike," said Brandon.

"Too bad," said Jack. "Now get to bed."

Doris poked Brandon in the ribs. "We'll have fun. You can help your old Granny."

He skulked toward the tent.

Later, Doris tried to get comfortable without strangling herself in the narrow sleeping bag. As a younger woman she'd taken pride in being a nature girl, but at sixty-two, her bones were already protesting the thin blow-up mattress, and she'd only been horizontal for ten minutes. It would be a rough night. What was she trying to prove?

She turned over again. In the dark, someone farted.

The next afternoon, after the hike had been cut short, Doris sat on the examining table in urgent care while the physician's assistant typed an essay on the computer. She looked like she was twelve.

The PA stood and tucked her clipboard in her armpit. "So like I said, use calamine where we pulled out the cactus, and alternate ice and heat for the muscle pull."

"Yes, I heard you." Doris buttoned up her slacks and climbed off the table.

The PA raised her hand. "Wait a minute. Before you go, how much do you exercise?"

"I'm thin. I don't need much."

"That's not what I'm asking."

Doris glanced away. "Okay, never."

The PA nodded. "This is the kind of injury that occurs when

a body's out of shape."

"Thank you so much for that assessment." Doris reached for her purse.

"You're going to hate old age if you don't take care of yourself."

"In case you didn't notice, I'm already old. It's too late."

"It's never too late."

"How would you know?"

The young woman smiled. "Since you're sedentary, you'll need therapy for a few weeks, maybe more, depending. What kind of insurance do you have?"

"None, obviously, or my son wouldn't be paying my bill."

"There's a low-cost gym in most cities. I'll have the nurse find one near you. It's not pricey. They charge based on what you can afford."

"In that case, it will be free."

When Doris got home she found a notice in her mail, warning her that she was late again on her mortgage. As if she didn't know or was somehow in danger of forgetting the fact. She dropped the plastic bag they'd given her at the clinic and leaned against the kitchen counter. Most of the time she could buck up and manage what had become of her life, but sometimes, like now, it overcame her – this listlessness, this weight pressing down on her so hard that it was almost impossible to stand. Somehow she made it across the kitchen and into a chair.

After three days of hauling her aching body around on a bum leg, Doris made a path through the mess in her driveway and backed the Buick out of the garage, barely avoiding a high-speed collision with the Big Truck. The truck's window rolled down and a disembodied hand flipped her off before the truck roared away.

At the gym, which was overheated and smelled vaguely of mildew, Doris approached the desk clerk. The girl looked up briefly from texting, gave Doris instructions in a spurt of monosyllables, and then returned to her phone. Picking her way through a roomful of sweating female weightlifters, Doris found an empty treadmill and began to walk. Her body hurt all the way down to her toes, but after a few minutes she got distracted with CNN on the TV overhead, even though she had to squint to read the captions. No one spoke to her, for which she was relieved, because most of the other patrons sported tattoos and face metal.

After ten minutes, the treadmill next to her began to move. Doris glanced over to see a pale young woman in a faded kerchief and grayish-pink sweats. The girl's hair was stringy and blond, and her face glistened with sweat. She fanned herself and smiled over at Doris. "My thermostat's all out of whack. I'm on chemo."

"I'm sorry to hear that." Doris turned back to the TV, hoping the girl wouldn't talk anymore. She wasn't used to strangers confessing their medical problems, and the girl interfered with her solitude. With eyes on Wolf Blitzer, Doris pointedly ignored her.

"Yeah," the girl said, "it's pretty tough, but I'm hanging in."

"Good for you." Doris offered a tepid smile. Glancing sideways, she saw the girl was hanging onto the side bars and biting her lip. "Are you all right?"

"Some days it's all I can do to get out of bed, but I think it's better if you stay positive, so I'm trying."

"Do you need anything?"

"No, thank you," the girl said in a whisper.

Doris turned back to Wolf, who reported that the President's ratings were tanking. As if anybody cared about that in real life. Working out at a seedy gym when you don't know if you'll be homeless in a month changes your perspective.

The girl spoke again, but Doris pretended not to have heard. She pushed the button to make the treadmill go faster.

"Ma'am? I need to tell you something."

Doris' sneakers slapped more loudly and she kept marching until her heart was pounding out of her chest and she had to slow down.

"Excuse me, can I tell you something?"

Resigned, Doris pressed the pause button. She needed to catch her breath anyway. "Yes?"

"There's a big pile of bird poop on your left shoulder."

Doris craned her neck. "Good Lord."

"Let me." The girl picked it off with a tissue, scrubbing at Doris' tee shirt to get it clean. When she finished, she wadded it up and tossed it in the trash.

"That was nice of you. Thanks."

"You're welcome." The girl looked depleted.

"Do you need to sit down?"

When she nodded, Doris helped her to the ground. The girl had a strong odor, and Doris wondered if it was the chemo. "I'll find you some water." She returned with a cup and held it out to the girl. Her eyes were mismatched, two slightly different shades of green.

"I'm Lisa, by the way."

"Doris. How are you feeling?"

"Better. Maybe we could go to coffee sometime, and get to know each other," Lisa said, taking tiny sips.

"Maybe." Doris stood. "Well, if you're okay–" She climbed back on the treadmill and pushed start.

"Thanks again."

Doris didn't answer.

For the rest of the week, she avoided the Y, but by Monday enough time had passed that Lisa would probably have forgotten the coffee idea. Doris made her way through the grunting, weight-clanging women and found a treadmill. After her workout, during which Lisa never appeared, Doris felt so good that she stopped for milk and day-old bread on the way home.

The next day, she went back to the gym, and the next and the next, until two weeks later, trudging toward the end of mile five on the treadmill, Doris' relief turned into concern. What if Lisa had taken a turn for the worse? Did she have family or friends? She looked dirty. Maybe she was homeless. Doris increased her speed and focused on Wolf. Lisa never showed.

When Doris pulled into her driveway that afternoon, Austin Stonebreaker was waiting for her with several envelopes. "These were delivered erroneously to my address."

She took them from him. "The mailman is usually pretty good."

"Not in my opinion. I typically receive two or three items a month not meant for me. It's the unions. They foster complacency. That's why I'm voting Republican this year." Stonebreaker held out a sign to her, a shiny new duplicate of the one he destroyed. "However, in this country, you have the right to champion whatever nimrod strikes your fancy, and I apologize again for my rash behavior."

Doris stared at the campaign sign and then him. The man was fighting a smile.

"I regret having lost my temper," he said, "but it was almost worth it. You should have seen them at your candidate's office. I shall forever treasure their misplaced look of hope."

They glanced up as the familiar roar signaled the approach of The Big Truck. Doris felt the reverberation through her feet, and a minivan barely avoided a collision as the Truck raced through a stop sign.

"Someday there will be a tragedy," said Stonebreaker.

A week later, Doris was up to seven miles on the treadmill. She was about to leave when Lisa walked in. Doris hit the stop button and stepped down. "I wondered where you were."

"You did?" Lisa dropped her gym bag. It looked big enough to hold a body. "I was evicted. Now I'm living down at Maple Street."

"The park?"

"It's not so bad. They leave the bathrooms open all night." Lisa swayed. Grabbing for the handrail, she sank down to the belt of the treadmill.

"When did you eat last?"

Lisa put her head between her knees. "Don't remember."

Doris grabbed for her gym bag and pulled out a granola bar and a bottle of water. Lisa unwrapped the bar and explained between bites.

"I was living with my sister, but when her husband wanted back in, she was afraid to say no. So I had to leave."

"That's terrible." Doris sat down on the other treadmill. "Can you get an apartment?"

"I'll find something," Lisa said. "I get a little from the state. Disability," she said, eating the crumbs off her shirt. "It's not much but I manage."

"All that and cancer, too," said Doris. "You're an admirable girl."

"What else can you do? You have to keep living."

"That's what I'd like to think, but it's hard." Doris couldn't help it. Her story tumbled out. By the end of it she had an idea. "Why don't you move in with me? I wouldn't charge much."

"Are you sure? Oh, my God. Seriously? I would love that."

"Don't you want to see the house first?"

"I'm in no position to be picky," said Lisa. "Anyway, I can tell from your aura that it's an awesome place."

"It is awesome. My house is in a safe neighborhood. You'll like it." Doris pointed at the bag. "I'll help you carry it to the car."

"There's something I have to do first. Can you give me a couple days?"

"Sure."

They embraced, and Doris liked it, even though Lisa smelled rank.

"When you're ready, call me." Doris scribbled her number on a scrap of paper. "I'll come pick you up."

At home, Doris felt a weight lifting. She hadn't wanted to admit it, but she'd been lonesome, and now with Lisa moving in, she'd have companionship and purpose, plus a few bucks. She might be able to keep the house. She called Jack with the news.

"No references? She could be an axe murderer for all you know."

Doris clutched the phone between neck and shoulder as she wiped the kitchen counters. "She's not big enough to lift an axe, and she has cancer."

"So you're going to be her caretaker? How will that work?"

"You're overdoing it."

"Maybe so, but I recommend you have her obtain a bond in case something happens."

"For crying out loud." Doris said goodbye and hung up. As a tax attorney, Jack lived in another world. He had no idea what she had to do to survive, and this Lisa situation was a ray of hope. Doris shouldn't have expected him to understand.

All week, she cleaned and straightened. In spite of misgivings, Jack helped her by hauling away the junk in the driveway. She vacuumed and scrubbed, feeling newly energized. She hadn't noticed how scruffy the place had become; Lisa's impending arrival was already yielding benefits. Doris put fresh bedding in one of the guest bedrooms, one of several with its own bathroom and shower.

On Friday night, the house sparkling, she fixed herself a wholesome dinner of soup and salad. Afterward, she watched television, not even minding the commercials. Soon, she'd have company. They could watch shows together, and comment on the plots and characters. Doris wondered how much education Lisa had had.

In the distance, she felt a vibration rumbling under the floor. Doris, thinking it was an earthquake, looked around for a place to duck and cover. The rumbling got louder, and tires squealed in front of the house, followed by a bloodcurdling yelp. Doris threw on her robe and ran outside. In the light of the streetlamp, she saw the Big Truck sneaking away, and the unmoving body of the retriever. The family next door spilled into the street wailing, the children loudest of all. Doris comforted the mother while the father, after covering the dog's body with a blanket, carried it to the car.

The next morning, Doris pounded on Austin Stonebreaker's

door. Surprised, he invited her in. She accepted coffee in a china cup with a floral pattern and gold at the rim.

"They were my wife's," Austin said. "A bit feminine for my taste but still useful."

"They're very nice." Doris set the cup down. "I need your help."

"The Board has tabled any action, as your property has been cleaned up."

"It's not about that." She clasped her hands as if praying. "I'd like to borrow a gun."

"Pardon?"

"I know you have guns. I saw your NRA belt buckle."

"Why do you need a gun?"

She told him about Angie.

"That is a shame."

"Yes, and the next time I see that truck, I want to shoot the tires out."

Austin refilled her cup. "There are a dozen reasons I wouldn't recommend it. For one thing, you can't know the consequences. What if he wrecks the truck and kills an innocent bystander? What if the bullets hit something else? They could go through the tires and penetrate the walls of a house."

Her chin dipped. "She was such a good old dog. Next time it could be a child."

"I have a better idea." He went to the garage and returned with a toolbox.

That night, she dressed all in black and joined Austin in his Jeep. They waited for the Big Truck to drive by, and when it did, they followed, not an easy task given the Truck's proclivity for running stop signs and even red lights. At the edge of town at a motorcycle bar, the driver screeched to a stop and hopped out. Seeing him, Doris snorted in surprise. The man was barely five feet tall, and as round as a beachball. He was bald, with a fringe of long hair and a wispy goatee. He wore sunglasses, even thought it was dark.

As soon as he disappeared inside the cinderblock building, Austin eased his Jeep close behind the truck.

"Unscrew the stem cap, stick this into the valve and give it a twist," he said, holding out the tool.

"Me?"

"Either that or you drive the getaway car."

Doris eyed the stick shift; she hadn't driven a manual transmission in forty years. "Give it to me."

Austin slapped the tool into her hand. She slipped out of the Jeep and crept to the front tire of the truck. Knees protesting, she got down low and followed his directions, applying the tool to the first tire. With a loud gush of putrid air, it emptied in seconds. Doris peeked over the fender but saw no one, so she moved to the back and repeated the procedure. The tire sighed in release, and the truck leaned sideways like a tired old horse. Doris snuck to the opposite side, her joints screaming, and emptied the two remaining tires. Pocketing the valves, she leapt back in the Jeep. She and Austin exchanged high fives and drove away laughing like teenaged vandals. That night she lay in bed, happy to imagine the trouble she'd caused.

However, another week passed with no word from Lisa. Doris fretted, worried the girl had lost her phone number or run into some kind of trouble. Doris increased her visits to the gym, hoping to run into Lisa there, but no luck. After five days she asked at the desk.

"Didn't you hear?" The clerk popped her bubble gum. "They found her body in a hotel room. She was OD'd."

Doris closed her eyes. "That poor, poor girl. Her circumstances must have driven her right over the edge."

"Circumstances?"

"Being homeless and having cancer."

"Breast cancer, right? That was one of her plays. That or MS, or sometimes kidney failure. Everybody down here knew that. She was definitely somethin' to watch."

Suddenly too fatigued to do anything other than drag

herself back out the door, Doris returned home and lay down on the sofa. She flung one arm across her face, wishing for sleep, but given it wasn't even lunchtime, sleep failed her.

Still, Doris remained prone, thinking. Life was a wonderment, was it not? Everything could look a certain way, and then, one instant later, completely the opposite, and both perspectives were true until they weren't.

She opened her eyes. A brown stain had appeared in the corner of the ceiling, as if the roof had begun leaking, a fact she'd failed to notice since the last heavy rainstorm two years ago, right after Harry left her.

That evening, she sat on her back deck, watching the lights wink on downslope as she polished off another glass of wine.

"I warned you," said Jack, sipping his beer. "No offense, Mom, but you need to get serious about your situation. I have a friend who's a realtor. I'll have him call you."

Doris didn't answer. In the western sky, the orange haze faded to pink, then purple, then black.

The next morning, Austin awoke to the sound of hammering. He looked out the window and saw Doris pounding a sign into her lawn. She tested the sign for sturdiness, returned to the garage and closed the door. Austin shook his head. The sign said, "Rooms for Rent."

~ 12 ~

THE NEW COUNTRY

To be defiant about age may be better than despair - it's energizing - but it is not progress. Actually, after fifty, aging can become an exciting new period; it is another country.

--Gloria Steinem

Marlene pulls on her navy blue blazer, jumps into her Kia sedan and floors it. Traffic is light. She gulps coffee from her travel cup, changes lanes, and spills on her leg. It burns like hell, but the spot blends into the dark polyester and is forgotten. The office manager has called everybody in early this morning, saying it's all hands on deck. One of the clients is going down, a big corporate account, and the partners are panicking.

Arriving at the parking garage, Marlene checks her hastily-applied makeup and discovers a big clump of mascara has fallen from her lashes onto her cheek and now it's smeared. She licks a tissue and scrubs it, doing the best she can in the dim light. Cursing, she grabs her purse and hurries into the building, heels clacking, the big toe on her left foot throbbing with arthritis.

This isn't the Saturday she had planned. The list taped to

her refrigerator – replant African Violets, try new Weight Watcher's recipe, return slacks to Target – will have to wait.

On the way to the conference room she notices one of the aging attorneys has shaved his head to accommodate increasingly noticeable hair loss. Now he stops at the front desk and allows the cooing receptionist to caress his shiny skull.

"So sexy," she purrs.

Delighted, he cocks his hand like a pistol and, winking, fires at her. He pivots toward the conference room, nearly flattening Marlene.

"Jeez!" he says.

"Sorry." Marlene follows him into the conference room. Her preferred seat along the left wall has been taken, forcing her to sit near the windows. Here, the angle of the light will be unkind, magnifying her wrinkles and any chin hairs that may have sprouted overnight.

She sits down and crosses her ankles. Marlene wears a pantsuit. More than one associate has referred to her as Hillary.

The room fills with suits and skirts. While they wait for the founding partner, a young associate finishes her makeup and shoves the cosmetics back into her bag.

A young man watches. "It must be hard to be a girl."

"No, it's fun." Her spidery lashes, shellacked with chemicals and glue, widen. "I feel lucky to be able to wear makeup. I mean, men can't. They have to be who they really are."

The senior partners parade into the room on the heels of the founder.

"All rise." Nobody stands. It is just Tyler joking around. Tyler, the most ass-kissing of the associates, is lobbying for partner. If he doesn't get it this time, they'll toss him.

"Boys and girls, we're in trouble." The founder, elbows on table, frowns. Or tries to. The man has been experimenting with Botox. The paralegals laugh behind his back because he is so old and ugly, why bother?

The founder explains that their client, a CEO battling a

sexual harassment claim by a dozen women employees, has been secretly filmed trying to put his hand up the skirt of his mail room clerk. The video has now gone viral. "Ideas? Anybody?"

The partners lean forward, pens drumming against antique cherry wood. The associates scribble on yellow pads, frantic to come up with the winning calculation that will catapult them to partner. The smell of coffee, cologne and B.O. fills the room.

"Give them Jane Wallace," says Marlene. Heads swivel toward her. Faces, at first uncomprehending, clear up at once. The logic is unassailable.

"Jane Wallace, yes!" A young associate leans forward, squaring her shoulders and blocking Marlene from view. "I propose we simply acknowledge that mistakes were made, and cut a check for Ms. Wallace. Then the whole problem goes away."

Marlene's face burns. "That's what I just–"

"Brilliant!" The founding partner beams at the busty young associate.

"Thank you, sir."

"But I–"

The partner's great head rotates toward Marlene. "Did you write that down?"

"Yes, but it was my–".

"Fine." He glances at his watch, which costs more than Marlene's car. "Get a summary to us right after lunch." He stands. "All right, people, back to work. Let's make this Wallace thing stick." He strides out of the room, followed by the senior partners, followed by the junior partners, followed by the associates, followed by the assistants.

Marlene remains alone at the table. This is the third time this month an attorney has stolen one of her big ideas. They have learned to hover nearby without making eye contact. Like seagulls off the back of a fishing boat, they wait for her to fling a piece of wisdom from her vessel. Marlene knows she should be more careful, but she is tiring of the fight. After all these years, she is still only a paralegal, which is fine with her, but she would like a bit of recognition, maybe even the same raise everyone else got last spring instead of a measly letter of commendation for her file.

"You going to sit there all day and feel sorry for yourself?" Tina, the office manager, leans in the door.

"Leave me alone."

Tina laughs. "You have no one to blame but yourself. How did you expect them to act? They're attorneys."

"I will never get used to it."

"You're too sensitive, Miss Priss. And where's that cost analysis I asked you to do?"

"Check your inbox once in a while. I sent it to you yesterday." Marlene hauls her tired body out of the chair and heads back to her cubicle.

At dinner, she opens a bottle of cabernet someone gave her for her sixtieth birthday. She sits at her small dinette and drinks the entire bottle.

That night she has vivid dreams in which she can lift off and fly simply by spreading her arms wide. She soars like a frigate bird over rich cropland and fragrant orchards. When she lands in a city and resumes her human shape, people move aside in deference. Her hair flows in crinkly silver waves down to her waist.

When she awakens on Sunday morning, Marlene feels strangely buoyant. In the bathroom mirror she flinches at a stranger, but no, it is her. Marlene's bottle-brown hair has inexplicably turned gray in the night and grown six inches. Her eyebrows are thicker, big and bushy. Her nose is longer, hawk-like, aquiline. She turns this way and that, admiring her newly-fierce profile. Her biceps are like iron, her thighs powerful. For breakfast, she eats a pound of bacon, six eggs, and a half a loaf of bread smeared with butter. Instead of going to the gym she wipes the spider webs off her bike and rides fifty miles.

On Monday morning, she discovers nothing in her closet fits. Everything is too small for her muscular new frame and too short for her new height. In the back of her closet she finds a rust-colored number from Chico's that flows like a ceremonial robe. She tops it off with ropes of bold, ethnic necklaces that she bought years ago in Sedona but never had the guts to wear.

In the bathroom she fluffs her hair until it fills the room with silvery light. At her elbow is a wicker basket full of eye shadows, lipsticks, mascara, eye liner, concealers and revealers. Marlene tips the basket into the trash can. Then she opens the drawers under the vanity and throws away her exfoliators, hydrators, masks, scrubs, soothers, moisturizers and conditioners.

Arriving at the office, her beads clack along with the slap, slap of her old Birkenstocks on the marble floor. Attorneys gape and cower. Secretaries linger and peek, curious. Partners stare, speechless and unhappy.

In her cubicle, she leans down and, with one arm, sweeps piles of documents and records into the trash, for she has no need of paper. She can see and remember everything ever written or recorded on those documents. She lights a candle and waits.

An attorney appears at the doorway to her cubicle. He hesitates, unsure.

"Speak," Marlene says.

"Do you remember my request from last Thursday?"

She gestures at a chair.

The attorney looks over his shoulder, then sits. "My client is losing faith. If I don't win this case, he will take his business to the competitor, and I will be fired."

"I understand," she says. "I will tell you what to do. Follow my directions to the letter and you will win the case."

He nods and bows. "Thank you."

He follows her directions and wins. Soon all of the attorneys are lining up outside her door, waiting to receive guidance, eager to feed on success. She works shorter and shorter hours, but on the occasions she deigns to appear at the office, she wears voluminous capes in bright colors and is greeted with swarming deference. Her cubicle fills with plants, tendrils, feathers and spirit catchers.

One day, the founding partner appears at her doorway and asks for a moment of her time. "I have a big problem." He shakes his head, fingering his mustache. He shifts from foot to foot, waiting to be invited to sit. His loafers reflect the candle light in her cubicle. "This case is national – and if we lose – publicity, reputation, financial ruin…"

She listens, her eyes fierce behind her nose. When he is finished, she stands. Closing her eyes, she turns to face the north, east, west, and south. She opens her eyes and glares at him. "Here's the news," she says. "You must do this and nothing but."

"I don't think–"

"Correct. Don't think. Do." She shoves him out into the hallway and sits in her recliner. Soon she is snoring. Attorneys and secretaries tiptoe past her cubicle. When she awakens she demands chocolate. Minions rush to bring it in two-pound boxes stored in a specially cooled vault.

On the day the verdict is announced, reporters camp outside the office, trying to interview Marlene. She appears on television, and bloggers begin calling her The Crone. Her secretary starts a Facebook page. Soon she has eleven million followers on Twitter.

The founder gives up his corner office with a view of the ocean, so she can be more comfortable. He provides her a car and driver so that she may conduct business at her convenience. Corporations line up to hire the firm where they may benefit from the wisdom of the Crone. She becomes a frequent commentator on CNN.

One day the President of the United States calls, seeking help with the Middle East.

Do this, the Crone advises, and do it exactly. The president follows her advice. Within days, Palestinians rejoice, Israelis share bread, and Iranians recite poetry in her honor.

The Crone builds a mansion on a cliff overlooking the ocean. She dispenses wisdom and conducts encounter groups.

Following her example, older women everywhere begin to wear flowing robes made of organic material in bright colors. They adorn their graying hair with feathers and jewels and wear comfortable shoes. They laugh and drink wine at lunch, and eat dessert instead of dinner, and they watch, eyes full of sympathy as young women struggle with high heels and unformed thoughts, not quite ready to explore the new country.

ESSAYS

I included these short essays about midlife and beyond because as you know, it's not fiction. Real life intrudes. The essays that follow are intended to suggest some possibilities for a new perspective in the second half.

~ 13 ~

BEING OPRAH

What would it feel like to be Oprah? No, I'm not talking about living in a fifty-million-dollar house near Santa Barbara (for which she wrote a check), or having a private jet to haul you anywhere in the world, or your own TV show and magazine and cable network. No, I'm talking about something else: the attitude. What would it feel like, to feel like Oprah?

This question occurred to me as I unfurled a big anniversary issue of O Magazine. On the cover, Oprah stands next to a giant cake. She's been on the cover of every one of her magazines since the very first. That must be almost two hundred issues. She is the only face of O, blow-dried and airbrushed to within a pixel of perfection.

In this anniversary issue, she is even on the back cover. In a special nod to her anniversary, and forgoing what must be tons of advertising revenue, Oprah is portrayed in a lovely silhouette. She is wearing diamond earrings and a sparkling, sequined dress. The picture lacks any text, as if words simply fall short.

Now, you might think I'm going to say that Oprah's ego is way over the top, but I'm not. I'm asking you to suspend judgment and think about how it would feel to be that person on the back cover. Imagine you had the power to decide to occupy that space, and then to direct the stylists and the artists and who-knows-who-else to focus on one thing: making you look fabulous. Imagine your one-point-five-million subscribers and countless other readers gape-mouthed in awe when they see you on that page. Can you feel it?

Me, neither. It's too much of a stretch from my normal life, and the self-negating attitudes many of us struggle with. So let's do a warm-up exercise, after which I'll ask you again.

I was dining alfresco on El Paseo recently, El Paseo being the Rodeo Drive of the Palm Springs area. It was high season on this mid-winter day, and when I looked up from my croissant I saw that the Bentleys and Rolls Royces had cruised to a stop, and the shoppers had turned their backs on Tiffany and Cartier. Everyone was watching a tall, thin, forty-something greyhound of a woman, her long limbs clad from shoulders to toes in bronze leather, her coppery hair cascading down her back. Stunning, even for El Paseo, this woman who strutted past high-end showrooms, absolutely riveted on her own reflection in the plate glass windows. She seemed oblivious to us, the commoners who had themselves dressed up for this pricey resort area. For her, the only two people who existed on the street that day were herself and her reflection. Everyone ogled her – some scowling, others with mocking grins, some just shaking their heads. Lady Godiva and her horse wouldn't have gotten a better response. My own reaction was mirth: what a showboat! What an ego! How could a person act like that?

And then I felt a thrilling rush, almost a sense of vertigo as some unpredictable part of my mind took the question literally. Mentally, I left my fellow gawkers behind and hungered to feel like her, even for just one minute – to sit inside her mind and look outward at the world from her vantage point. Was she aware of us and feeding off our reaction? Society teaches us to be modest, and that braggarts and showoffs will be punished, but what if her parents taught her something different? What if she came from a culture where beauty was accepted as a gift from the heavens rather than a sign of conceit? Maybe she assumed that we adored her, and negativity never crossed her mind. How would it feel to stand so tall and strut so proudly, not only not minding the attention but inhaling it, your heart expanding with joy from your own reflection, and from all that human energy focused directly at you?

I ask you, could the sun shine any more brightly?

And then, as I stepped away from judging this woman – as I quieted the voice inside that whispered "narcissist" and instead simply admired the pure brilliance of her self-confidence, I felt freed from the bonds of jealousy, of envy, of competition. I felt like a spectator, admiring a fiery thing of beauty, and more than that, I felt lifted up, equal to that beauty, because I had the capacity to celebrate rather than denigrate.

Now back to Oprah.

We're all familiar with Oprah's history, how as a child she lived in a shack without running water, and that she was sexually violated before she was even out of elementary school. You might say she's overcompensating for a childhood that would have ground most of us into the dirt, that she's not really happy, and that nobody who is that driven could be, deep down. If she were happy she'd have married Stedman by now, right?

But I asked you not to judge.

Imagine that you built a media empire in which you launched, or boosted into the stratosphere, the careers of Dr. Phil, Suze Orman, Dr. Oz, Gayle King, trainer Bob Greene, fashion guy Adam Glassman, or genius thinker/advice giver Martha Beck, and countless other celebrities, authors, philanthropists and do-gooders. Oprah has won awards – *thirty* Emmys for her TV show alone. She has created thousands of jobs, given away vast sums of money and helped so many causes, small and large. She is a trailblazer, having been feted for becoming the first of her gender or race in many areas. She has funded schools and built an academy for poor girls in South Africa. Nelson Mandela loved her. Maya Angelou wrote poems for her. President Obama and Michelle consider her a friend. What must that feel like?

Oh, and the money? At the time of this writing, Oprah was bringing home $385 million a year. Her net worth was upward of a couple billion. Forbes identifies the source of her wealth with this most sterling of American descriptors: "self-made."

If I were inside Oprah's head – if I were her – and I looked in the mirror as I got ready for bed at the end of a long day, and thought about the weary necessity of tomorrow's schedule – a dozen meetings, a hundred decisions, camera/hair/makeup – I might feel lonely. I might feel the burden of leadership at the top of my media empire, and the hard-won distance from my childhood and youth.

But after I washed off my makeup and saw my plain, wide-eyed face stripped clean, my hair unstyled, my earlobes unadorned, I might let my shoulders relax. I might break into a grin. I might even say to the mirror, "Damn, girl, you're amazing!"

In our own humble (or astounding) lives, we are all accomplishing great things, even if it's only getting out of bed and showing up for work at a horrible job, because our family needs to eat. Even if it's only because we manage to keep a smile on our faces when dealing with damaged and demoralized family members. Even if only because we've managed to hang onto our houses for one more day.

Damn, girl. You're amazing.

~ 14 ~

YOU LOOK MAHVELOUS

I was standing in a mini-mart the other day waiting to pay for gas. A beautiful young woman in front of me was complaining to the cashier that even though she's thirty, she always gets carded.

I said, "It's because you've got a face like a peach." It just flew out of my mouth, and then I was glad, because she got it. The girl's eyes got real big and her mouth opened in this gigantic smile as she thanked me. For a second I thought she was going to hug me. Is it so rare, that one woman would compliment another?

Recently I was walking out of an office and a woman was walking in, and we held the doors for each other and then laughed, and as I went through, I told her the truth: "You look wonderful." She did. She had gone to a lot of trouble on her hair and makeup, and her outfit and jewelry were to die for. "Thank you," she said, beaming. I think when you hand someone a spontaneous, honest compliment like that, it's so unexpected that you get extra mileage out of it. Maybe that's because the recipient knows in her gut that a total stranger wouldn't say that unless it was sincere.

I read about this a long time ago, in a now-defunct magazine called "Lears – for the Woman Who Wasn't Born Yesterday." The writer said she was standing on a street corner in NYC, and this woman marched up, dressed to the nines, very tall, very put together, quite intimidating. Everybody was watching her, and her eyes were narrowed, as if daring someone to whistle. She stopped next to the writer, who said, "You look magnificent."

The ice princess melted.

Of course we're afraid to compliment strangers; we're perpetually on guard, but this is what makes a genuine compliment all the more wonderful. Go ahead, take a chance. Tell another woman she looks great. Say it with conviction and a smile. Yes, it takes a bit of courage, but why not generate a burst of positivity in the world? The worst she can do is snarl at you, in which case you'll have a story for all your friends. The best is that you'll feel great about yourself all day long.

~ 15 ~

WHY CAN'T WE DIE LIKE DUDLEY?

My brother and his wife recently put their beloved German Shorthair to sleep. Dudley was ready. Bro said Dudley told them when when it was time, and they put him on a blanket in the yard and gave him the blue juice (my sis-in-law is a veterinarian.) I am sure they petted him and cried, but it sounds like a pretty good way to go. Dudley died with the sun on his flanks, the smell of grass in his nostrils, and the love of his family all around him. I wish we humans would permit each other such a sweet farewell.

Of course, that's not how we do it, because human life is more valuable than dog life, and the risk is too great. Instead, we pull out all the stops to keep each other alive in spite of great illness, pain and struggle. Or at least that's how the general public handles it. Doctors? That's another story.

In an article entitled *How Doctors Die* by Dr. Ken Murray, we learn that doctors are so averse to the normal life-saving techniques visited on the dying that they even go so far as to have No Code (i.e., no CPR) tattooed on their bodies. Here is one reason: did you know that in order to properly conduct CPR on a patient, ribs are usually broken? How'd you like your old mom to have to deal with that?

I have had more surgeries than your normal midlifer, and were it not for these surgeries I'd have been dead several times over. I must I have a bod that's inclined that way, so I think about things like this, and if I were to receive an untreatable diagnosis, I'd forego all the extreme measures and enjoy the rest of my time on earth. What a privilege to have enough advance notice that you could organize your files (shutting down all my online accounts would take days!) and lay the groundwork for sending your loved ones off into the future comfortably instead of torturing yourself with toxic chemicals and premature hospitalization.

Of course, the problem is that medical knowledge is incomplete, and we can't often say with a high degree of certainty that all efforts are useless and we may as well go quietly, but if I were lucky enough to get such certainty, I think I'd rather get the blue juice. Wheel me close to the window, hook me up to the morphine, and *adios, muchachos*.

I hope I didn't bum you out but I believe this topic deserves more attention. Now that I've raised the issue, I'll drop it. The sun's coming up, the day is young, and we've got livin' to do.

~ 16 ~

DO YOU LACK PURPOSE?

After we retire, we sometimes lose our way. People who are working fulltime, and especially those who are also caring for dependent family members, don't have this luxurious problem. But if you're lucky enough to have a lot of free time, you sometimes feel guilty, as if you're wasting your days. Lethargy swamps you. You can't seem to move forward. You need a jolt, something to wake you back up.

At one time in my life, I felt that way. I was between careers and drifting. I thought of signing up for some kind of mindfulness retreat, a weeklong camp for indolent introspective old farts. And then my mom asked if I would help her get back to Indiana to see her dying brother-in-law. It was early December and she was too frail to go alone. We were gone a week, during which time I lived with, and like, my sick and elderly relatives. This experience snapped my head around. By the time I got back, I felt reborn, newly grateful for the world of possibility in which I lived.

But if you don't have a week, you might attend a funeral. Preferably of someone you don't know. Blunt, I know, but hear me out.

I used to be a professional funeral-attender. Like a US Vice Prez, I dutifully attended numerous services, representing my employer during my thirty-year career. Although I didn't suffer as much as those who'd lost a loved one, it was still hard to see them grieving. After a couple hours, I could leave, and I would feel a guilty appreciation for my own more fortunate circumstances. I was alive. My child was well. I had a job, and a roof over my head. Life seemed blessed. Gratitude restored.

Or, lacking available funerals (or if you are too classy to attend as a voyeur), you might help out at your local elder care facility. Mom spent three weeks in one while recovering from a broken leg, and I visited her twice daily. There was always something to do; straighten the room, make sure her water jug was refilled and necessary supplies within reach, chat up the employees. These places are always understaffed and an inmate can go hours without a drink of water. Walk out of there, my friends, and you'll feel like turning cartwheels for the great gift of independence.

You don't know how free you are until you survive cancer, a car accident, terrorist attack or heartbreak you thought would flat kill you. At your age, you've already gone through some of that. If you're feeling brave, you might close your eyes and let your mind drift back to those harsh times. Visualize those days when you were suffering. Remember how it felt to be paralyzed by illness or grief? Now open your eyes, grab a hanky, and blow. Good God – you're still here! You're okay. For the moment, you're safe, and you have the world at your feet. What are you going to do with it?

~ 17 ~

COULD YOU LIVE IN A DITCH?

My relatives did. Circa 1880, when my peeps first rolled into North Dakota on the cross-continental railroad, they were chasing after free land. Land was precious, because they had run out of it back home in the Banat section of Lets-Call-It-Germany (the politics shifted so much it changed every five minutes, from Austria to Hungary to Turkey.) In order to claim the land on this virgin prairie – so full of potential - you had to build a house of some kind, but there were no trees.

It was prairie! A sea of grass as far as you could see, maybe fifty miles in every direction from the little knoll under your feet. Without trees, how would you build a house? You couldn't buy lumber – there were no towns, no lumber yards, no Home Depot. Heck, no neighbors, doctors...Besides, you would have spent most of your money on a horse, plow, seed and provisions. There was nothing left for a house, and anyway, a house was just a place you slept when you weren't trying to coax crops out of the rocky fields. (Of course, this was the farmer's view. His wife and half-dozen kids might have felt differently.)

So to start with, the farmer dug a cave into a hillside, put up a front door of some kind and went to work. Eventually as a farmer's situation improved, he would build an above-ground house made of blocks of sod, like a dirt igloo. They called them soddies. When the farmer could, he built a new and better house out of rocks. You can still see these stone houses all over North Dakota.

But not everybody prospered, and not everybody moved into better digs (maybe that's where that word comes from?) A couple of my bachelor uncles liked it so much they never moved out. Sometimes in the winter, this could be a problem, as snowfall could block their door. Other relatives would always remember to go dig them out as soon as the storm stopped.

I loved researching my novel. I've made a couple of trips back to ND to experience the land, the people, my relatives, and my history. Reading about the immigrant experience was fascinating. That's part of why it took me so many years to write the book. You can get lost in the research. Even if Dakota Blues were never published (perish the thought), I am a richer person for the experience of writing it.

~ 18 ~

LET'S RETIRE THE "HOW NOT TO ACT/LOOK/SOUND/GET OLD" ARTICLES

I was reading a blog for women over fifty. Said blog included a 10-part series called "How Not To Look Old." Also, *More Magazine* runs that crap all the time, and I'm appalled that we're buying it. It's like we're still in junior high, reading *Seventeen* and slavishly following its mandates, afraid to show the slightest bit of independent thinking.

We're so brainwashed to abhor age that our efforts to emulate youth is accepted, expected, and admired. We demand it of ourselves and each other.

Of course smooth skin is beautiful, but I refuse to try to have it, or to lament that I don't have it, or put some eighteen-year-old on a pedestal because she does have it. I also refuse to see myself as less-than because I have wrinkles, lines and crevasses. My belly looks like a road map of scars from life-saving surgeries. If that's the price, I'll take it.

My elderly mother is wrinkled and her spine is bent, but she attends exercise class three times a week, drives herself all over town, enjoys lunch and movies with a large group of girlfriends, and is still hungry to learn, grow and evolve. All of these women are successful at being old. They're courageous and enthusiastic, in spite of the physical and mental pain that old age layers on. Yet when they go to the store they see the magazine stands plastered with headlines about how much we desperately do not want to look like them. Is that the news? Is that what matters?

I'll tell you what matters: in 2010 I had a scare, in that a CAT scan indicated the possibility of the form of cancer that killed two of my aunts. Although the surgery (yes, more scars!) revealed no cancer, after that experience, I don't really care if I look old – I'll just be glad to *get* old.

About the Author

Thanks for reading my stories. I hope you enjoyed them, and in any case, please feel welcome to leave a review on Amazon.com. Your opinions are important and your feedback helps me decide how to go forward with future works.

I'd like to invite you to visit my Amazon author page at **http://amazon.com/author/lynnespreen** (no capital letters). There, you'll find my award-winning midlife novel, *Dakota Blues,* and the sequel, *Key Largo Blues*. Also, I'd love to see you at my website, **http://www.AnyShinyThing.com,** where we chat about issues facing people at midlife and beyond.

I'm a former corporate suit who was fortunate enough, after a thirty-year career, to reinvent myself as a writer at the age of fifty-eight. I'm also a mother, grandmother, wife, golfer, gardener, and social media addict. I live in Southern California and am a member of the Diamond Valley Writers' Guild. If you're in the area, come join us.

Best wishes in finding your own true path to happiness.

66178281R00092

Made in the USA
Middletown, DE
05 September 2019